Missing Girl

Piper Punches

Copyright © 2014 by Piper Punches

Cover Design by Martin Hammond

ISBN: 978-0-9910936-3-2

eBook ISBN: 978-0-9910936-2-5

First published in the United States in 2013

For inquiries, please contact the author directly at:

www.piperpunches.com

piperpunches@gmail.com

DEDICATION

To all the missing girls.
May their families find peace and may we someday bring all the
missing girls home.

CONTENTS

NOTE TO READER

The sex trafficking industry is thriving right under our noses. Whether you live in a major city like Los Angeles, Miami, New York City, or Chicago or you live in a small Midwest town with a population of 500, you are living amongst individuals that profit off the sale of women and children. It is a practice that does not discriminate based on geographical location. Although there are industry hot spots in the world that contribute in greater amounts to the sex trafficking industry, it is a global threat to the safety and well-being of women and children.

I feel it is important for the reader to understand that this industry is not limited to border towns like Tijuana or Nogales, both of which play a prominent role in *Missing Girl*. Sex trafficking is not indigenous to second or third world countries. In truth, it is the indulgence and excessiveness of first world countries that allow the industry to thrive as it does. Sex trafficking would not exist were there not people willing to pay to strip women and children of their humanity.

When reading Missing Girl you may question the authenticity of the situation. You may ask yourself, *How could she let this happen? How could she go along with this?* When you find yourself thinking these things remember that sexual slavery and human imprisonment take many, many different forms. This story tells a fictional account of just one young girl's journey into hell. There are countless real-life victims that may tell a different story, but each story should be given the credence that it deserves.

To learn more about how sex and human trafficking affect our global community, please visit The Polaris Project at http://www.polarisproject.org/.

Piper Punches

PROLOUGUE

In life my name was Sophia Lucia Cruz. In death it is simply *missing girls*. Not even singular, but plural, as if there was never one single part of me that was unique or separate from all the other girls that were buried in that harsh Mexican dirt; victims of circumstance, irrevocable choices, and just plain bad luck. If I still had the capacity to cry, I would, because it is that sad and tragic. But when the knife slid deep into my belly and the blood gurgled at the base of my throat I knew that tears wouldn't save me and they won't change my story now.

Why am I here? You don't believe in ghosts, do you? That's okay. I didn't either before I became one. Even when I was a little girl and I insisted I saw my *abuela's* ghost at the foot of my bed, knitting me a blanket that had all the colors of the rainbow, I let myself be persuaded that ghosts were a figment of my imagination.

"Sophia," my mama said as she smoothed my hair and planted her lips on my head. "My sweet Sophia, close your eyes. Whatever you think you saw was a shadow. Just a trick of the moon." She would then sing me a song and rock me back to sleep.

I wish I could visit mama at the foot of her bed tonight. I wish I could tell her this isn't her fault. She did the best she could. She should forgive herself. But I can't. Instead I am stuck here; wherever here is. It's somewhere between the dark black Mexican night and its brilliant sunny days. I am simply hovering above what remains of my body. People, family members, loved ones, sometimes the police, make their way to these dusty fields with picks, sticks, and shovels, hopping to discover the remains of their missing girl, but most of them find nothing and end up leaving the fields more distraught than when they arrived. Isn't it twisted the way that families are forced to come to these fields of death with hope and expectations of finding their loved ones? I am not judging and I certainly don't blame them. But when they leave they leave hopeless because they know that they will continue to be left without answers - without a body to properly bury. Because let's face it: when the missing leave they never return.

I'm there. I can see me - or at least what is left of me. Some of the girls – and men, too – that are buried (can you even call it that?) here were merely stabbed, shot, choked, or suffocated and then haphazardly tossed like garbage into this death dump. Not me. Although no one would come looking for me and I wasn't anyone important, my kidnappers had left their marks branded on my skin and this made me identifiable and a risk even in death. Unlike some of the other bodies buried around me, I was dug a deep enough grave that I wouldn't be noticed right away. This would give the lime that had been sprinkled over my body time to work its decomposing magic.

How can I talk about my demise so casually? I don't know. Perhaps that is the beauty of death. I am removed not only from my physical body, but my emotions are flat-lined as well. However, I still feel compelled to tell my story, so there must be some emotion that lingers, even though my soul has released its grip on my human form.

Why am I compelled to tell this story? I guess because no one else will. Most people don't want to tell stories with tragic endings, but they need to be told, otherwise they are forgotten. I want you to know who I am. I want you to know I am so much more than a poster that has been damaged by wind, rain, and time. I don't want to be so easily dismissed. I want you to know that I was so much more than a missing girl.

CHAPTER ONE

"But Mama," I protested as she scooted the laundry basket across the kitchen table towards me. It was brimming with two weeks' worth of Mama's worn out delicates and my brother's dirty gym clothes. "Why do I have to go today? You know the laundry mat is shady any day of the week, but Friday nights are the worst."

"Do you have other plans tonight, *chica*?" Mama asked, setting a trap that I couldn't avoid. My lack of response was the answer she expected.

The late September heat that had settled in the valley was suffocating. Mama wiped her forehead and turned away from me, but not before I saw the skid marks of perspiration that had been left behind on her forehead. With her back to me she pulled her long chestnut hair up into a messy bun on her head and I caught a glimpse of the sweat stains that had formed under her arms, turning her light pink shirt nearly red. In the past week the air conditioner had heaved one final breath before dying and our wash machine followed suit. We didn't have money to fix either so we were left to sweat in our soiled clothes.

Mama sighed as she looked out the window that overlooked our neighbor's overgrown, weedy yard. It was one of her complicated sighs that was infused with frustration and regret. "Sophia, I need you to do me this favor."

"Why can't we use Mrs. Jeffries machine?" I whined like a two-year-old. Mama had always said teenagers were like toddlers only taller and mouthier. I was only acting the way she expected, I told myself.

Mama turned around. "Because Mrs. Jeffries is an old woman, her home is rank, and our clothes would leave there dirtier than they were before they were washed. And," she added one more pair of Jesus' foul gym socks to the top of the pile as a punctuation mark to her point, "because it is not Mrs. Jeffries responsibility to take care of us."

Mama walked away leaving me in the sweltering kitchen pondering the point. I felt like shit. Really, I did because with Jesus and me in the house it shouldn't always have to be Mama's responsibility to take care of us. I was 17-years-old and Jesus would be 15 in two weeks. We were capable of being helpful, responsible children. We were also capable of being complete and total asses.

Begrudgingly, I snatched the laundry basket off the table, tucking it under my arms, breathing out of my mouth to avoid the stench of Jesus' socks. It didn't help. With my free hand I grabbed my cell phone out of my back pocket and texted Hayden. *Meet me at the laundry mat? Earning my keep, I guess.*

I waited for her to respond outside of the house, sitting on a lawn chair Mama kept near the front door. It was her smoking chair, she said. While she didn't care if she destroyed her lungs, she certainly wasn't going to go down for killing her kids with second hand smoke. The chair was one of those old lawn chairs from the 1980s with weaved fabric that frayed and fell apart too easily. This chair was green and yellow, faded from the sun.

I tapped my foot and waited impatiently for Hayden to text me back. She was the only friend I had whose parents allowed her to come to my home. Mostly I was a pariah; someone that was looked down upon for having a heritage that wasn't fashioned from diamonds, Mercedes, and Vera Wang. I can't say that it was discrimination. I lived in Mission Valley, an area of San Diego that was rife with Hispanics and last names like Rodriquez, Garcia, and Sanchez. Of the 800 teenagers that attended Vista Linda Senior High, Hayden, whose skin was whiter than the porcelain toilet in my bathroom, was the minority. The problem wasn't the light, cafe color of my skin or way I tried to adopt my mother's accent even though I was a born and bred American. No, the problem was that the tiny section of the universe I inhabited was downright dangerous. Any parent in their right mind wouldn't let their kid come to this neighborhood that was littered with shells from stray bullets and riddled with drug dealers that divided their time between here and Tijuana. Hayden was only given a wide berth because her parents cared more about their stock portfolios and fancy parties than paying close attention to the whereabouts of their daughter; her assessment, not mine.

My phone vibrated against my thigh. *Can't. The parentals are being particular tonight.* She ended the short text with a sad face emoticon. I put my phone into my back pocket and shrugged off the letdown. The sun hadn't set yet. It wouldn't for another three hours. I had plenty of time to get back home before it became suicidal to walk alone.

The screen door to my house slammed. Mama walked up to me and placed her hand on my shoulder. She kissed my cheek and looked into my eyes. We shared the same eyes. She always told me I had my Papa's sturdy features, but the eyes we shared. "I love you, Sophie. Be safe. If I didn't need your help, I wouldn't ask you. I've got some business to take care of tonight. Okay?"

I didn't ask what her business was, although I suspected it was visiting Mr. Debold. Although Mama had invited him to dinner several times over the course of the past several years and he behaved himself in a halfway decent manner, he wasn't a gentleman. I had seen the way his eyes looked me up and down, filled with carnal indecency. It was gross and disgusting, but what was sicker was the way he eyed my Mama. I had caught him grabbing at her ass when he thought I wasn't looking. Mama didn't shoo him away, but she wasn't responsive either.

I began to put two and two together about a year ago when I noticed that after Mr. Debold's visits things started showing up in our house that we couldn't afford. First it was the dishwasher. Next, Jesus was able to attend the soccer camp he had begged Mama to send him to for almost three months. I finally realized the extent of my Mama's and Mr. Debold's relationship when the Honda Civic materialized in our driveway. Taking care of business meant visiting with Mr. Debold to get the air conditioning fixed and the wash machine in working order again. Sending me to the laundry mat was part of the plan.

I leaned my forehead against Mama's and released her of a little guilt. "It's okay. Sorry I'm being a little shit."

Mama smiled, patted my cheek, and pointed her finger at me. "Language, little girl. You talk like that and you won't ever find your way out of this inferno of poverty. You understand?"

"*Si*, Mama. Don't worry about me. I'll be fine."

Mama smiled, satisfied with my answer and walked back into the house. That would be the last time I ever saw my Mama.

CHAPTER TWO

My papa left us when I was six years old. Some people may think that I was still young enough to not be affected by his absence, but those are the same people that believe in the Easter Bunny and rose-scented shit. I may have been barely able to write my name, but I knew how to spell abandonment. It was spelled P-A-P-A.

Papa's desertion was wretched. Most people believe that when a person, especially a parent, abandons the people they are supposed to love that it is for the best in the long run. This is because most people that take the coward's way out were never invested in the relationship to begin with. But Papa was. He was a devoted father that used to sit with me at the kitchen table and put together puzzles that seemed to have no solution; leaving us both perplexed and insistent that the puzzle makers were playing a cruel joke. He would sit with me in his oversized recliner that had come from the dumpster outside of La Tienda de Delgado. And, even though he had spent nearly three days deep cleaning its upholstery with a machine rented from the grocery store, Mama pitched a fit every time she walked by it claiming it was filled with vermin and sin. Papa always laughed heartily and hoisted me onto his lap anyway so we could read a book together.

The day he left was like any other. The sun rose on schedule. Mama took me to school, holding my hand, reciting simple math facts that I was supposed to memorize. Jesus trailed behind us, complaining that he wanted to go to school, too. When I walked out the door with Mama and my brother,

Papa was sitting at the kitchen table doing nothing remarkable or memorable. He kissed me on top of my head like usual and ruffled Jesus' hair. He kissed Mama on the mouth and twirled her hair in his finger. Did he linger a little longer than usual because he knew this would be the last time? Not that I can remember. Everything seemed right as it should be. Then it wasn't anymore.

He left the house after we did (at least that's what Mama had theorized) with nothing more than his wallet and the clothes on his back. Why did Papa leave? Well, your guess is as good as mine or Mama's. For weeks she had pounded on the doors of friends' homes demanding to know where Miquel Cruz had gone. Was it drugs? Another woman? Rumors circulated through the neighborhood that Papa had made acquaintances with *polleros*; human smugglers that brought people across the border that were searching for a better life. Was it possible? Sure. Anything is possible, but it didn't make his disappearance any easier to deal with, because we all knew if he had crossed the *polleros* or had gotten caught smuggling illegals himself, a bullet between the eyes was a given.

During the initial weeks of Papa's disappearance, Mama became smaller. She cried constantly. She worried even more. She couldn't go to the police. Not with her status and not with Papa's either. If she filed a missing persons report, she would be flagged and ripped from our lives as fast as Papa had been. All she could do was pray and bother the neighbors with questions that had already been asked and answered. Mama had set up an altar in our front room embellished with a blessed rosary, her wedding ring, a picture of Papa and Mama on their wedding day, and candles that stayed lit eternally. If Jesus or I would blow the candles out or extinguish them as we ran by, Mama would pitch a fit, make the Sign of the Cross, relight the candles, and spend hours praying.

When Papa left Mama was only 25, but grief and despair ages a person rapidly making them nearly unrecognizable in their own skin. It was around this time that I noticed traces of gray weaving their way through her hair that no longer shimmered in the sunlight. The skin under her eyes darkened. She rarely touched food, so her natural littleness quickly transformed her into a skeletal creature.

After a while, she couldn't keep the candles lit any longer; not on the altar and not in her heart. She knew that Papa was never coming back and she was the one left to deal with what he left behind; a family that was severed, but repairable if she tried. And Mama did try. She worked hard to provide as much as she could for Jesus and I. She left Mexico City when she was only 15 to come to a land that she believed would give her more opportunities than the brothels and machismo men in her neighborhood could offer. If she had started a new life for herself then, she could do it now.

I knew how Mama paid for things like soccer camps and my quinceañera dress. It didn't take a genius to figure out that she was trading sex for money, even if it wasn't considered her day job. It was her supplemental income to offset the measly wages she received cleaning houses for families like Hayden's; those families that had spare bedrooms, granite countertops, and in-ground pools. Did knowing this about my mother make me love her less? How could it when it was love for me and Jesus that drove her to sell her humanity for a bank account that wouldn't fall short each week?

Everyone sells themselves for something anyway, don't they? At least in this neighborhood they do. Teenage girls that should have been writing in diaries and listening to their iPods while helping their parents with dinner wore low-cut tops and barely-there shorts to attract the attention of boys that would never treat them well, but were something to cure the boredom that accompanied being poor in Mission Valley. The boys weren't any different. They may not have strutted around half-naked, but they wore their pants low, spoke in a language that was the dialect of the streets, and sold their childhood for a chance to hold a gun or make a grand selling a good time to kids aching for an escape from the monotony of adolescence. So, yeah, everyone sold themselves for something because it was the only way that they could feel in control of their destiny, even when it was clear they were simply puppets being manipulated by an unknowable puppet master.

***

As I suspected the laundry mat was teeming with filth and all the machines were taken too. I flopped down in a plastic chair that was bolted to the floor. Really? Were plastic chairs from the seventies that hot of a commodity? Closing my eyes, I listened to the swishing of the clothes in the dryer and the loud, incessant rap music that radiated like toxic material from a parked car that meant no good. A small child whined, while the smell of its rank, dirty diaper assaulted my nose and the sound of a hand on sweet, baby flesh made me cringe. As much as I hated spending my Friday night at this cesspit it was a reminder of how good Jesus and I had it at home.

I smelled his cologne before I heard him say my name and I tensed. "Sophia, baby! What's the likes of a sweet *chica* like you doing here?"

Regretfully, I opened my eyes to find Manolo Castro standing over me. His skin was the color of mocha; darker than mine even though his mother was an Irish woman who had made the mistake of marrying a hard-headed Mexican who believed in administering the hand of force whenever anyone disagreed with him. We used to play together when we were toddlers. Mama was friends with Maddie, his mother, for a short while, which meant we were forced to sit in our living room side by side and pretend that we were thrilled to be in each other's company. Even as a child, Manolo was mean spirited. He would purposely rip the heads off my Barbie dolls and pull at my hair, making me cry and cower in a corner. Complaining to Mama was pointless because she chalked it up to a term of endearment. Endearment my ass. Manolo was just a mean son of a fuck and not much had changed as he grew taller and developed facial hair that was as believable as a 1960s porn star.

I didn't answer him. He could go screw himself. Thankfully, a machine opened and I brushed past him. He followed.

"Baby girl, why you got to be like that? Didn't we have ourselves some good times way back when? How've you been?"

God, I thought. *Was this place always this hot?* My hair was clinging to the back and sides of my neck, strangling me with sweat that seemed relentless and unwilling to let go. Manolo stood on the other side of the machine I was using, sizing me up and letting his eyes linger too long on my chest. I dumped the entire basket of clothes, colors and whites, into the machine all at once. I could care less if the colors bled. So what if Mama got mad? Because I had to wait for a machine to open the chances of getting home before the sun set were diminishing. I had to get out of here as soon as possible.

Was it a premonition? Some might say that I sensed the danger, but there wasn't anything to sense or predict. Everyone knew Manolo was bad news. I was simply being logical.

Manolo shrugged and fished around in his pocket for a cigarette. As he lit the cigarette, he shook his head. "Guess *tu madre* didn't teach you proper manners."

I huffed, crossing my arms in front of me. "Guess your Mama didn't teach you how to dress. Wife beater, gold chains? You couldn't afford a belt?"

"Have to dress the part, Sophia."

"Of what? A thug?"

Manolo smiled. "A mover and a shaker, *chica.*"

"The only thing you move is white powder and your finger on a trigger."

"I see word has got around that I get things done."

I stared into his black eyes and saw my reflection; the fear was clearly exposed on my face no matter how smug I tried to be. *Little girl*, I told myself, *you are playing with fire and out of your league.* Leave it be and go home.

"Where's your brother tonight, Sophia?"

I didn't like the tone to his voice. "I don't know."

"You sure he isn't out near the park riding his bike? He seems to really be trying to perfect his BMX moves lately." He took another drag off the cigarette. Instead of blowing the smoke away from me he leaned across the machine that separated us and let the smoke plume envelope me. Not one to back down, I held my breath and fought the urge to gag.

"Your little bro and me need to have a conversation."

"I doubt that."

"Don't matter because I know where to find him. Just thought it would be better if he came to me." Then Manolo laughed. He threw his head back. His Adam's apple prominent and protruding. "You have no clue."

"About what?"

"Jesus."

I watched him carefully, anticipating his words and his moves. The heat that had penetrated the air around us suddenly cooled. The sweat that had formed on my neck became like icy fingers sending chills throughout my body.

"You need to leave, Manolo."

"Not until I get paid."

"We don't owe you money."

"Like I said. Jesus and I need to have a conversation. He's skimming off the top and I don't like it."

"Skimming off the top? Jesus isn't a dealer."

"You sure about that?"

Jesus had a tendency to act out and he had been causing Mama some grief lately. But drugs? No, it couldn't be true. Jesus knew better. He was taught better.

"Maybe we can work out a deal." Manolo offered.

"My mama taught me not to make deals with the devil."

Manolo smirked. He walked around the machines and stood in front of me. He was nearly six feet tall, skinny but still imposing enough to overpower my five foot frame. He leaned down and brought his lips to my ear. He raised the hemline of my shirt with something hard and cold. It wasn't until I felt the tip of the blade tease my flesh that I realized what it was. "I'm not the devil, baby. I'm a fucking god. You're gonna play this little game with me or I am going to hunt Jesus down and gut him like a pig. I'll even make you watch."

People always think they know what they would do in a situation where their fate is determined by the next step. They always say they would run away, scream at the top of their lungs, or kick the person in their balls, but they really don't know what they would do. Logic gets twisted when cold steel is against your skin and someone you love is threatened. When this happens you make deals. You offer up whatever you have to the devil and pray to a lost God that you will be saved. You walk away from unwashed clothes and get into a car with a person you know has no intention of letting you go because everyone sells themselves for something. You watch them smash your cell phone into tiny, jagged pieces, knowing that you will never be found because protecting the ones you love matters more. Everyone can be bought; you just don't realize it until you've been offered a deal.

CHAPTER THREE

When I was eight I decided to run away. Where I was running to I wasn't quite sure, but anything had to be better than the sad house that still smelled like Papa's cologne when I walked by Mama's room. On more than one occasion I had witnessed her sprinkling the amber liquid on her bed. When I saw her doing this, I was tempted to run to her, cling to her legs, and wipe the tears from her cheeks, but I held back. Letting her know that I witnessed her heartbreak felt disgraceful. Even at eight, I realized that people need to be left alone with their sorrow.

Running away didn't prove to be as difficult or unrealistic as I thought. Mama had started working longer hours and was rarely home before eight o'clock. She relied on Mrs. Jeffries and a handful of other neighbors to keep us fed, occupied, and alive while she worked. Some of our caretakers were actually tolerable, especially Jessie. Jessie was a college student who lived a few blocks away. She played board games with Jesus and me, let us fall asleep on the couch, and didn't care if we ate macaroni and cheese five nights in a row. I loved Jessie. She reminded me of Mama before Papa disappeared. She was playful and happy whereas Mama had grown tired and crabby.

But then one day she showed up at the house with a big ring on her finger. It flickered like magic and reminded me of a candy ring pop except it wasn't purple or green, but clear and ice cold. Jessie promised that she would stay with us even though she planned to have a fairy tale wedding and lead a fabulous new life with her handsome Prince Charming. Then one day she showed up with the ring still on her finger, but also with a swollen eye that was the color of ash and a lame excuse about why she couldn't stay with Jesus and me anymore. Mama accepted her answer, but I refused to look at her. Her broken promise meant that we would have to spend more time with Mrs. Jefferies who smelled like sulphur and made us eat our vegetables.

Although Mrs. Jeffries put on a good show when Mama was around, she didn't really pay much attention to us. She preferred to sit in front of the box television in our living room, flip through trash magazines, and watch television shows that made her cackle and slap her knee. This was why it was so easy for me to pack a backpack full of cheese crackers and fruit roll-ups for my planned escape, completely unnoticed by everyone. That is except for Jesus.

"Where you going?" He asked in his whiny six–year-old voice. He barged straight into my room and flopped onto my backpack. I yanked it out from underneath his skinny butt and glared at him.

"Be quiet," I demanded. "Go shut the door."

I expected Jesus to argue because he hated when I bossed him around, but he obediently closed the door then restated his question. "So, where are you going? I want to come, too."

"No, Jesus."

"Why?"

"Because I said."

"But I want to." His voice got higher and his chin started to tremble. His eyes were wide and dark, so dark it was hard to distinguish the pupil from the iris.

"Go play outside. Leave me alone."

"Why you have to be so mean?"

I ignored him and went to my nightstand. I grabbed the tiny prayer book that had been a gift from Papa for my First Communion. It was pure white with gold-stamped letters on the front and with the edges of the pages trimmed in gold, too. Sometimes Mama and I would read a blessing at night, but most times she was too exhausted to stay awake past the first word. So I would read the blessing to her the best I could while she dozed on my shoulder. I wouldn't be able to leave it behind.

When Jesus saw me remove the prayer book from the nightstand and slide it into the bag, he leaped off the bed. "I'm telling," he said. He started to run to the door. I grabbed him by the collar. He tried to wrangle free, but my grip was good and his resolve was weak. He offered a solution. "Let me come."

I let him go and put my index finger in his face. "You be quiet."

"Where are you going?" he whispered.

I turned away from him. "I don't know. Maybe to see the ships."

"That's where Papa used to take us."

"You remember that?" I asked without turning to look at him.

I hear him sigh. "Yeah, I remember."

"You were too little."

"I remember a lot of things, Sophia. I am not a baby. I want to come." He climbed up on my bed and traced the seams of my backpack.

I ruffled his hair, giving him my best smile. "Mama needs you. Besides, I won't be gone long."

"Liar."

"Whatever, Jesus, but you can't come. What do you think Mrs. Jeffries will do if she notices we are both gone? Huh? You have to stay to make sure she doesn't know I left."

He called my bluff. "She won't even notice. Besides, I don't want to stay with her. She calls me *Little Tonto*. I don't like it."

I giggled. "Little Tonto? What does that mean?"

Jesus rolled his eyes. "One of her stupid television shows. It has a guy in a mask that rides a horse and he has a friend that Mrs. Jeffries says is an Indian. She says I have brown skin like him so I am her Little Tonto. I don't even know how she knows what color skin he has because the show isn't even in color. It's in black and white. Boring."

Skin color shouldn't matter in a place like Mission Valley where people like Mrs. Jeffries were the minority. Everyone in our neighborhood was a different shade of brown, from different cultures and different backgrounds, but to people like Mrs. Jeffries we were all the same. Did she mean ill-will by her remarks? Probably not. At least that's what Mama would say when Mrs. Jeffries would make off-color, racist remarks, *She means nothing by it*, Mama would say. But it didn't make it any better. It still made you feel like you belonged to a group of people that could easily be lumped into a broad category: Indian, Mexican, Native American, Asian, black. To people like Mrs. Jeffries we were all the same; indistinguishable and forgettable.

"Just ignore her, Jesus."

"Come on, Sophia. Please. I promise I'll be good. Okay? I won't yell at you or call you a stupid, weenie head."

"You never call me that."

Jesus bit his lip and looked down at his lap. "Sometimes I do."

"When?"

"When you're being a stupid weenie head."

"Fine." I relented. "But you're carrying the bag."

Jesus gladly accepted the price for being a tag-along.

We made it as far as three blocks before Jesus ignored my warnings about running across the street. He thought he was too cool to hold my hand and almost got plowed by a city bus. A police officer was patrolling nearby and heard Jesus and I arguing and that was that. We were politely told to get into the patrol car and he took us back home.

Jesus cried all night long, upset and mad that he had foiled my plan. I climbed into his bed and pulled the covers up around us and sang the songs that Mama sang to me when I had a bad dream. As his breathing slowed and his mouth sagged with sleep, I knew that I would always protect him. I would never let anything happen to him no matter what. How could I have known then how much that promise would cost me?

***

From the time I was a baby to now my world was limited and miniscule. Rarely did I venture more than three miles from my home. I rode the bus to the mall and walked to the park to read under the trees. Once in a while Mama, Jesus, and I would drive to the beach and lie on the sand for hours listening to the roar of the ocean, watching the majestic waves of the Pacific Ocean break on the shore, but beyond that I didn't venture far. I certainly never traveled down Interstate 5 in rush hour traffic towards the border.

The border was off limits. Everyone knew what could happen to girls when they crossed the border. At this time of night, as the lights that lined the interstate illuminated the cars all around us waiting to gain entry into Mexico, I knew that I was going to be returning to home of my parents, my ancestral family. Under any other circumstances I would have been excited to leave my small world behind, but now I wanted desperately to return to my mundane life.

I glanced at Manolo. He started straight ahead, focused and seemingly unaware of me. He tapped his hands on the steering wheel to a song on the radio by a Latin American singer I didn't recognize. Mama played a lot of Latino music in our home, but I didn't quite care for the beat or the fact that they sang too fast for me to catch the words. Mama may have spoken Spanish fluently, but Jesus and I were Americanized. We could barely speak Spanglish correctly. As the car crept closer and closer towards the checkpoints, I wished I had taken the time to learn Mama and Papa's native tongue because I had no idea how I would communicate when Manolo let me go. Yes, I guess I still held onto some hope that escape or relinquishment was a possibility for me. Yes, yes. Silly girl, I know, but hope is the kidnapping victim's only solace.

As we crept along, getting closer and closer to leaving California behind, I thought about the missing girls that haunted the Mission Valley and the other communities in

Southern California. Living so close to Mexico was like living near a black hole. With so much violence emanating from the border towns, it was common for girls to disappear, never to be heard from again. Every once in a while a *gringa*, as Mama would call her, would go missing and the news would splash her picture across the television screen. Alerts would be broadcast if she was underage and everyone in the community would be instructed to be vigilant. The police would promise to do everything in their power to bring her home. When a Latino girl crossed the border the response was muted, non-existent in most cases. The reasons varied, but the sentiment seemed to be the same. *What's the point? They are back with their own kind. Let them go and may God be with them.*

I looked at Manolo again. I wasn't sure if God could protect me from ignorance and greed because I knew that was the only reason he took me. Was Jesus dealing drugs? I doubted it, but I couldn't take that chance. Manolo would tell people I went willingly. I knew his type. He would confess to nothing even though no one went anywhere willingly when a knife was pressed against their ribs. But it wouldn't matter. The only person who could protect me was me. First, I tried reasoning.

"We will never get across, Manolo. It doesn't matter what color our skin is. I don't have a passport. You forgot that little detail."

He laughed. "You forget that you are nothing more than a stupid *puta*. A little girl is all you are. That will change quickly, though."

"Why are you doing this?"

He said nothing.

"We used to play together, Manolo. Our mothers were friends. You are better than this."

His hands tightened on the wheel. "Be quiet, Sophia. That was a long time ago. In case you didn't notice, things changed. People change."

"Look, if Jesus owes you money I can get it for you. I'll

find a part time job and pay you back as soon as I can."

Manolo finally looked at me. I expected his eyes to be agreeable and friendly, a small amount of humanity showing through. Instead, I saw rage and a lost boy trying to be a man. Reasoning would not work with someone who had already sold his soul. "Yes, *puta,* you will work it off."

Immediately, I grabbed for the handle of the passenger door. Manolo anticipated my reaction. He pressed the automatic lock button, but I wouldn't give up that easy. With all the strength I could muster in my small body, I brought back my legs and kicked at his face. Harder and harder; I let the rage spill forth. Once or twice my foot hit the horn and I thought, *Surely someone will hear. They will help.* But no one acknowledged the car as it bounced up and down to the rhythm of the assault. Manolo's thick hands grabbed my ankles. He twisted. I screamed. I screamed as the pain sent fire through my nerves and into the back of my neck. I slid away from him, pushing my back against the door to get as far away from him as possible in the small space.

Manolo turned away from me, running his hands through his hair. "We all make choices, Sophia."

"I didn't choose this," I whispered.

"You didn't resist."

"You threatened Jesus."

"Sure, but you didn't believe me. You knew better than to believe Jesus would run drugs. But you still made the choice to walk away with me. Now sit up and get it together. A little bit of greasing and we will be through this border check no questions asked."

He was right. As I sat in the passenger's seat with my head down and my ankles throbbing, I listened to Manolo and the border officer converse in fast Spanish, laughing and carrying on like it was business as usual. Just before the border agent backed away from the car, he whistled softly and I could feel his corrupt eyes on me. "Got yourself a pretty one, don't you?"

Manolo didn't answer. Instead he rolled through the San

Ysrido crossing. When the United States was officially in the rear view mirror, he said, "You could have resisted. You could have let me slice you open and bleed out on the floor of the laundry mat, but instead you choose to be taken. You know what, Sophia? You may have chosen wrong."

CHAPTER FOUR

As the car lumbered along the streets of Tijuana, I leaned my head against the window and fought back the tears that were teetering on the edge of my lashes. I swallowed hard pushing them down into my throat, forming a lump of unshed tears that continued to grow like a cancerous tumor. Under any other circumstances, I would have found the landscape beautiful, but I couldn't move past the realization that life as I had known it had changed. It happened that quickly without much thought or consideration. Once this truth set deep into my bones, the lump of tears dislodged from my throat. My one final act of rebellion before being dragged from the car was to vomit all over the floorboards.

"Where are we?" I asked, wiping traces of vomit from my lips with the back of my hand.

"What does it matter? It's not like you're going to be sending any postcards home."

"Someone will come looking, Manolo. You won't get away with this."

"No one is going to come looking for you, Sophia. No one ever comes looking for missing girls once they cross the border. What makes you think you're so special?"

Manolo parked the car in a tight alley off what appeared to be the main thoroughfare. It was still relatively early in the evening, but the city's nightlife was already amped up. Music from various clubs pulsated out into the streets. Men lounged against storefronts, ogling women that were available for purchase. The men didn't have to try so hard and they knew it. Charm wasn't a currency accepted south of the border. A few people glanced at me, but their stares were vacant and uninterested. To them I could have been anyone; anyone but someone that would hold their interest for more than a moment. Already, I was starting to disappear.

We moved swiftly against the crowd, then Manolo pulled me into a dimly lit stairwell. One, two, three, four, five steps and we reached the top, to an inconspicuous door that had no number, but a sophisticated locking mechanism that seemed out of place for such a seedy area. Manolo pushed in a series of numbers. His fingers moved speedily across the keys. He didn't need a cheat sheet. He didn't pause to recall a number. This was not the first time he had happened upon this door.

Manolo pushed open the door and dragged me behind him. "Yasiel," he yelled to an empty apartment. "Yo, Yasiel, get your ass out here. I brought you a present like I promised."

A woman sat at the kitchen table. She didn't look up, but quietly addressed Manolo in an American accent. "He stepped out. Your payment is on the counter." She pointed to a bag of white powder that sat on top of a stack of bills.

"Yeah, that's what I'm talking about, *mamacita*." He walked over to the bag, dipped his finger into the powder, and took a taste. Next, he rolled up one of the bills and sprinkled the white powder on the counter. He leaned over the bill and snorted the powder fiercely. He offered the bill to the woman, but she dismissed him with a flick of her hand and an uninterested glance. He inserted the bag of cocaine securely into his shoe and tucked the stack of bills into the waistband of his pants.

As he brushed past me, he looked me up and down one last time. I stared back at him, willing him to have mercy on me. For one glimmer of a second, I thought he would repent. Instead, he looked back at the woman and said, "Take good care of this one. Don't let Yasiel mark up her face. See you around, Sophia."

When he left, I should have moved. I should have run

toward the door, but all I could do was stand in that strange foreign place stunned into muteness and immobility. I stood there for what seemed like an endless minute, listening to Manolo's footsteps descend down the stairs. When his footsteps were no more, the woman at the table jumped up so fast that the chair she had been sitting in toppled backwards, the cheap wood splintering into two distinct pieces. She rushed at me and instinctually I covered my head. Instead of hitting me, she thrust me towards the door. She never spoke, but with one hand firmly grasping the flesh of my upper arm and the other one on the door knob she shoved me out the door. But rather than delivering me from evil, she hurled me into the arms of one of the most beautiful men I had ever seen.

He looked down at me and smiled, and then placing his hands on my shoulders, he averted his gaze over my head at the woman standing behind me. I couldn't see her face. I could only hear her breathing. It was calm, but low and deep. It sounded like fear. That's when I looked up at the man's face again and realized that he was too beautiful to be visiting an unmarked, easily forgettable apartment tucked discretely away in a border town that was ravaged by greed, lust, and desperation. He was too beautiful to be here and that instantly made him horrifying.

CHAPTER FIVE

"Lizzie," the man spoke, slowly and purposefully. He shook his head in an amusing manner and made a tsk-tsk-tsk sound with his mouth as if he were scolding a child. "What were you thinking?"

He dropped his hands from my shoulders and walked over to the woman. He ran his finger along her jawbone and then pushed her hair away from her neck, revealing a jagged scar that hadn't healed well. It was about five or six inches in length, raised and puffy. As he leaned into her and kissed the scar on her neck, she closed her eyes. He then raised his eyes to meet the woman's and said, "If I weren't in your debt, I wouldn't hesitate to kill you."

The woman said nothing. She stood still as a statute, not reacting to his menacing words, leading me to believe she had heard these words before. I wondered how she had gotten that scar.

The man walked away from the woman and ignored me temporarily, giving me time to study him in greater detail so I could give the police an accurate description. Yes, again, I know – stupid, silly girl. I still hadn't fully accepted my predicament.

As he moved into the kitchen his tan suit pants moved freely. They must have been made of a fine material like silk or something similar because they didn't pull or bunch. They were nothing short of exquisite. His suit jacket matched his pants and although the apartment was sweltering there were no traces of wetness penetrating his suit. It was unnatural.

His hair was raven black, darkened deeper by the gel he

had combed through it. His hair was just long enough to be pulled back into a small ponytail at the base of his neck. It was a style that many of the boys in my neighborhood attempted to wear, but couldn't pull off. Under different circumstances, I would have found myself stifling a laugh because it would have reminded me of the time last year when Jesus had thought he could get away with wearing his hair this way.

Mama was not a fan of the ponytail, which she deemed trashy and counteractive to Jesus' intelligence. "*Mio*, you should wear your hair in a respectable style," she argued.

Jesus just dismissed her and went about disrespecting the world with his hairstyle until one day he came running out of his room at six o'clock in the morning with a stricken look on his face and a tiny nub of hair in his hands.

"What did you do?" he wailed like a three year old.

Mama smiled devilishly and held up her kitchen scissors. "I made you respectable."

***

It turns out the apartment was merely a drop-off location. Once the man, who I suspected was the Yasiel person Manolo had been yelling for, decided that the place had been wiped clear of any human traces, the woman and I were loaded into the back of a black van that smelled like rotten fish and urine. We sat on the floorboards, my tailbone aching every time we hit a bump on the road. After a few minutes of uncomfortable silence, the woman spoke.

"How did he get you here?"

"What?" I asked.

"Manolo. How did he get you?"

"I've known him forever - since we were little."

"So, you came willingly." A statement, not a question.

"No. It wasn't like that. He threatened – he threatened my brother."

"Why?"

"Said he owed him money for drugs."

She raised her eyebrow at me. "And you believed him?"

I looked down at the back of my hands. Of course I didn't believe him, but he gave me no choice. How could I take the chance?

"Stupid girl," the woman said.

I looked up at her, examining this foe or friend closer. She was definitely older than me, but by how much I couldn't be sure. Her skin was pale to match her accent and her hair was a blondish-brown. She appeared to be just another *gringa*, but when her bottomless, black eyes caught mine I sensed we shared a stronger ethnic connection than I originally thought.

"My name's Sophia."

She held up her hand. "I don't want to know your name. You should have called Manolo's bluff. That is his game. It's how he gets girls to Yasiel."

"What if he wasn't bluffing?" I countered. "How could I let him hurt my brother? Wouldn't you have done the same?"

The woman shrugged. "It would have been easier on your brother. A bullet right between the eyes; it would be over just like that. It won't be so easy for you. It's a different story for girls. We serve a different purpose in this war."

"What war?" I asked.

Instead of answering me she reached down and picked at her shoes. The veins in her arms bulged. I had seen this before. It was a side effect of injecting oneself with cocaine. There were kids at school that had veins that looked like they belonged to bodybuilders, while the rest of their bodies wasted away from the consistent drug use. She continued to ignore me, letting the silence build and fully aware that I was studying her. Finally, she spoke.

"I'll do my best to protect you from the worst, but I can't make any promises."

CHAPTER SIX

We traveled in the back of the van for what seemed like hours, never stopping. When I complained about being hungry the woman gave me an energy bar that tasted like bark. When I couldn't hold my bladder any longer she handed me an empty beer bottle and suggested I do my best to aim. The longer we were held captive in the back of that van the farther I felt from my family in spirit as well as distance. There was no way that anyone would ever find me. Is this what it was like to vanish? Is this what happened to Papa? Or was his fate like the woman presumed Jesus's would have been had he been taken instead of me – a bullet between the eyes?

As if reading my mind, the woman spoke my concerns out loud. "It's best to let them go."

I refused to look at her.

"It's hard, but it makes this life easier."

"Nothing about this life looks easy." I glanced in the direction of the front of the van and then to the steel doors just feet away from me.

"Don't think about it. It's worthless. You won't get far. We are in the middle of nowhere. A wild animal is safer in these parts of Mexico than you would be."

"Mama will come looking for me," I insisted like a small child trying to convince an adult that unicorns, the Tooth Fairy, and the Easter Bunny were real.

The woman sighed and pulled her hair to the side, revealing her scar again. I averted my eyes. "She can try, but nothing will come of it. She's undocumented, I presume.

That's why it's so easy for children of illegal immigrants to disappear without detection."

I ignored her, continuing to eye the back of the van, formulating an escape plan. But she spoke the truth and I knew it. It was why Mama couldn't do anything when Papa disappeared. She couldn't go to the police. If she had, she would have put herself at risk. If she filed a missing person's report on me she'd be risking her own deportation and where would that leave Jesus?

"Where are we going?" I asked

"Does it matter?" was the woman's reply. Her voice was staccato; not soothing like Mama's would have been if we were in a frightening situation. Maybe the woman was right. Maybe I should let Mama go because it would be easier to adjust to whatever was ahead for me. But if I let her go wasn't that admitting defeat? Was I really ready to let go of my life?

We traveled in silence for a little while longer. The woman slept with her head against the cold, hard floor of the van and I tried desperately to stay awake. Just when I was about ready to give into the overwhelming tiredness that seemed to have overtaken my body, the van stopped and the back doors were flung open.

The sun hurt, blinding and searing my eyes. I blinked rapidly like a newborn that had spent nine months in darkness and was now expected to embrace its fate. The difference was I wasn't being delivered into the arms of a loving mother. I was being yanked out of the van and delivered into the rough hands of a stranger.

The woman followed me on her own accord. There were no hands laid upon her or boots kicking at the backs of her calves telling her to move. Although she moved freely, I understood that the chains that bound her to my captors were invisible, but just as strong. The pain that I had glimpsed in her eyes since we met told me she loathed every moment of her existence.

The men that held me tightly by both arms were muscular and faceless, towering over me by at least a foot. They had covered their faces with black ski masks and they smelled like sour body odor. Each one carried what looked like a semi-automatic weapon in one hand, with a smaller handgun attached to a holster on the back of their jeans. The woman saw me eye the weapons and she shook her head. I ignored her. I wasn't going to use them just yet, but it was comforting to know if I put up enough of a fight I might be able to grab one of those guns and end it quickly. I wonder if I could have really done that? Could I have put the gun to my temple to save myself?

The thought was fleeting because the next thing I knew I was being thrown to the hard ground next to a metal barrel. A match had been tossed into the barrel creating an eruption of flames. As I struggled to regain the breath that had been knocked out of me, I tried to take in my new surroundings. The sights and sounds of Mexico's nightlife had been replaced with the quietness of the desert. Mountains and brown earth encircled me. There were a few green patches in the dirt every once in a while, but for the most part everything was barren and dry. Off in the distance, I spotted a cluster of buildings that looked like they might have belonged to a bigger city, but it was hard to tell. It could have been a mirage, the way that the building danced and floated in the heat waves that radiated from the desert floor.

I had no way of knowing then that the city that bobbled and danced in the distance was my future because the entire situation felt surreal and unreal. Wasn't I just sitting outside of my home texting Hayden and loathing my teenage existence because I didn't want to help out Mama?

One of the masked men nodded to the woman just as another vehicle pulled up behind the van. The man from the apartment got out of the car. He still had on his tan silk pants, but he had removed his jacket. He wore a crisp white shirt that would certainly soil when the dirt particles landed upon its pristine surface. He didn't seem to care or notice. He simply walked toward the woman and me with that dazzling smile on his face that turned sinister the closer he got. The woman looked over her shoulder, appeared to take a deep breath, and then turned to me.

"Stand up," she ordered.

Again, I questioned her loyalty to me. Friend or foe? But I would rather deal with her than the masked men and the well-dressed thug with the dazzling white smile. Her eyes never left mine as she patted me down. She reached into my back pocket and found a ten dollar bill and my student ID. I had forgotten that they were there. Spare change and an identity were things I quickly forgot about once Manolo had put the tip of the knife to my stomach.

She held up the ID and Yasiel plucked it from her fingers. He held it up and studied the words. "Sophia, yes? Such a beautiful name for an exquisite young woman. Tell me Sophia, how old are you?" The words that fell off his lips were spoken in perfect English; his speech as polished as his dress.

I didn't answer him and he didn't care. He simply nodded and tossed the card into the flames behind me; rendering me officially dead. There was nothing left that could connect me with my past. As the flames devoured the ID my soul went with it, leaving a shell to be taunted and played with against my will.

"Step aside," Yasiel said to the woman. What was her name again? Lizzie? I couldn't remember and I wasn't sure I cared.

"Yasiel, please, she's just a girl."

"Yes, one that will serve her purpose over and over again. Don't fight me on this." He held her gaze until it was clear she would bend to his will.

She moved away and hugged herself with her arms. She shook as if she was cold, but the fear in her eyes was that of a wild animal. It quickened my breath and made me alert that something was about to happen.

Yasiel stood in front of me. "Take off your shirt," he said.

I didn't respond and one of the masked men moved towards me. Yasiel held up his hand, halting the man mid-step. "Don't resist, *munequita.* Resisting only makes it worse. I'll ask you again. Take off your shirt."

I looked to the woman, but she looked away. Slowly, I raised the threadbare t-shirt with bleached out graphic designs over my head. It was one of my favorite shirts. A gift from Mama for making the honor roll during my freshman year at Linda Vista.

"That's a good girl, Sophia. Now undo your pants and take those off, too."

This is the moment that people begin to judge and I ask that you don't because you can't possibly know what you will allow yourself to be subjected to when life as you once knew it has changed. When you switch from living life on auto-pilot to just surviving the moment, your priorities shift, rotating swiftly on an invisible axis. At that moment, my priorities were to make it through this round of the game and move onto the next where there might be an escape route or an exit plan. So, yes, I obeyed. I removed my jeans, tossed them to the side, and stood exposed in my bra and underwear underneath the blazing Mexican sun. Yasiel snapped his fingers and the woman moved to his side. One of the mask men walked around me. I closed my eyes, bracing for the violation I was certain was to come. But, nothing could have prepared me for what happened next.

With my eyes closed, I heard the woman make a plea on my behalf one last time and then an agonizing pain pitched me forward into the woman's arms. I struggled to breathe and I clawed at the woman's face and hair, panting and retching at the same time. She held me in her arms as the pain intensified and the smell of burning human flesh assaulted my nose. As I looked up into her coal, black eyes, I caught the trace of a tear brimming on her lower lashes, right before agony rendered me unconscious.

CHAPTER SEVEN

I dreamed in color. Not dull, distressed colors reminiscent of family photos that have been smashed between the glasses of a forgotten, dusty frame for way too long, but vibrant, unnatural colors. They were the types of colors that you would expect to find when watching an old, black and white movie that had been colorized to attract an audience more inclined to play a mindless game on their smartphones or tablets than to sit down to watch a family classic like the *Wizard of Oz*.

In my dream it was snowing; flakes as large as marshmallows floated down from the sky. When they touched my skin instead of melting they bounced off of it, rolling uncharacteristically away from me as if taunting and laughing at my silly idea that all snowflakes melt when they touch hot, human flesh. But what did I know? It wasn't as if I had ever seen snow in person before. Obviously, I was familiar with the white, fluffy stuff that looked like unflavored cotton candy, but I had never had the opportunity to touch it, taste it, or play in it. Living in Southern California didn't provide much occasion to get an unexpected snow day. If you wanted to see snow you had to travel north or west to find a mountain range with snow white, peaks and that wasn't a possibly for me.

The scene in my dream was blinding. The sun was suspended high in a flawless blue sky. Its rays reflected off the pure white landscape, creating prisms of light that pirouetted all around me. The sight was so exquisite and spectacular that I thought for a moment that I was in heaven;

that this was the light that everyone talked about. I started to walk towards the center of the light, but then I realized I was looking down at myself – not my present self, but the child version of me standing in the snow dressed in a puffy winter coat the color of a cherry red Popsicle. It was a coat that still hung in my closet back at home, a childhood memory of a missed opportunity stuffed between skinny jeans and tank tops.

The coat had been an unexpected gift from Papa. He had brought Mama and Jesus similar coats for a trip to the mountains. "My children should have adventures," he insisted when Mama opened her mouth to protest. "Grand, American adventures! What is more adventurous than exploring the Rockies?"

Mama had stood in the middle of our living room, holding her puffy purple coat that made me think of Barney the dinosaur to her chest, giving Papa a strange, curious look. Never had she been anywhere in her years that would have been cold enough for such insulated, restricted clothing. "*No dinero, Miquel.* We don't have the money for such a trip. Not for any of this."

Papa had grabbed Mama excitedly by the shoulders and kissed her ferociously on the forehead. The kiss was so forceful and filled with such passion that it left a red mark like lipstick on her skin when he pulled away. Papa was elated by his idea and Jesus and I were, too. We bounced around like Sumo wrestlers in our new coats, jumping around and in between our parents, excited to be going on a vacation. Other children went on vacations with their families, but not us. The biggest adventure we had in our short, young lives was visiting the ships yards and sucking on juice boxes while Mama and Papa dug in their pockets for enough change for a return trip home on the trolley.

"We cannot afford to not live life zestfully, Mari!" Papa exclaimed. Then he too began to bounce along with us making Mama laugh. She grabbed onto Papa's wrist and kissed him full on the mouth, something she avoided doing in front of us. She seized the moment to be happy.

We never made it to the mountains. Papa disappeared several days after the happiness and excitement, but in my dream the four of us were trampling and trouncing through the snow. This is how I was certain I was dreaming and not yet dead. Papa might have been gone, but I knew Mama and Jesus were safe and sound back home.

My five year old self rolled in the snow in the cherry-colored coat, making snow angels and delighting in the way the snow shaped and formed into various shapes and sizes. Papa and I built a snow fort where we hid playfully from Mama and Jesus, but accidentally made her cry because she thought the snow had gobbled us up. We had snowball fights and made a snow family that was too perfect to exist outside of a dream world. Then, like dreams do, the scene changed abruptly.

Instead of being in a snowy forest, we were in a world of ice. I could hear carousel music coming from a short distance away. Everything suddenly felt different. Instead of feeling elated and comforted like I had in the snow, this ice-world felt ominous. Papa turned to us and I thought he would tell us to run and hide, but instead he said, "What's life without adventure?" Then he put his finger to his lips and motioned us to follow him as he led us towards the music.

As we walked, the snow that had gathered on my coat started to drip, absorbing my coat's dye and creating what appeared to be a blood trail behind me as we walked closer and closer to the music. We walked a little further before reaching a pond that was frozen solid all the way through. The ice was immaculate and clear as glass. About a hundred feet from where we stood there was a carousel sitting atop the ice playing the tune that was both haunting and beautiful.

"I wanna ride!" Jesus squealed.

"Me, too," Mama said.

I started to run with them towards the carousel, but that's when I noticed the carousel was occupied. There were masked figures riding on top of the lions, the seals, the pandas, and the unicorns. At first glance, I only saw the masked figures that were holding their guns at their sides, but then I glimpsed that frightening white smile. It temporarily blinded and paralyzed me. When my sight returned and I was mobile again, I watched in slow motion as my dream melted into a nightmare.

Raising their guns, the masked men aimed for Papa, Mama, and Jesus as they ran, seemingly oblivious, towards the carousel. I tried to scream; to warn them; to save them, but my lips and tongue could not form the words. I was forced to witness the bloodshed as one by one the men took my family down. As the lone survivor, I stood in the middle of the frozen pond, mesmerized at the sight of the ice turning red from my parents' and brother's blood, waiting for the men to aim their guns upon me – a frightened little girl in a coat that had lost its color. Instead of killing me the men vanished into thin air. The only person left on the carousel was the man in the tan suit, smiling at me with his finger to his lips, hushing me.

Then the carousel exploded into flames and I was surrounded by fire and ice. The man in the tan suit towered above me, a monstrous figure with horns and scales covering his body and human flesh dripping from his mouth. He floated above the fire, laughing and taunting me until I was yanked out of the nightmare and brought back to the lair of a real life devil.

CHAPTER EIGHT

For three days the woman took care of me and tended to the raw wound on my lower back, soothing it with shaved ice and aloe, slathering thick coats of topical antibiotics on it with gentle fingers. Whereas I thought my assailants were trying to kill me, it turns out they were only interested in branding me. As I laid on my stomach on what appeared to be an old Army cot, the woman sat beside me, brushing my tangled hair, and singing lullabies to me that reminded me of Mama. For seconds at a time, I forget that I was a prisoner with a fate yet to be determined. Sometimes the lullabies were too much. I wanted to tell her to stop, but I didn't want silence either. This is when I would turn away and let the tears slide down my cheeks, the salty liquid pooling in the corners of my mouth.

On the fifth day, the woman brought me a white cotton dressing gown and fresh undergarments, instructing me to put them on. I had been lying on that cot with nothing on my ravaged body but my soiled t-shirt and underwear for days. It was the first time she had actually spoken directly to me since the incident in the desert.

"It will feel better against your skin," she said as she handed it to me and turned away.

Reluctantly, I slipped out of my clothing and watched her throw them in the trash. They were the last remnants of home, but to her they were nothing. I didn't say anything at first. I simply eased myself onto the cot and looked around at the room. "Where am I?"

She motioned for me to pick up the sandwich sitting on a

tray table next to the cot. Had I even eaten in the past few days? I couldn't remember. All I remembered was waking up from my nightmare and being given a bottle of tequila with a straw in it and told to drink; that it would numb the pain. It was the first time I had ever tasted alcohol and it was horrible. I faintly remember pushing the bottle away, but the woman insisted I swallow. I obeyed and passed out within what seemed like a very short time.

All I knew now was that I was hungry. As if on cue, my stomach growled loudly and I saw the woman smile. She had a beautiful smile. Her teeth were straight and white. They looked out of place in this dingy room that seemed to be held together by despair and a bad plaster job. When she realized that I had seen her smile, she scowled and turned away.

"Your name is Lizzie, right?"

"If that's what you want to call me," she said.

"That's what he called you."

She turned back to me and again motioned to the sandwich that I hadn't yet picked up. It was peanut butter and jelly – strawberry jelly. It tasted like heaven and I didn't really even like peanut butter and jelly. The way the peanut butter stuck between my teeth and the roof of my mouth had always made me want to gag, but I ate the entire sandwich in four bites.

"It's best not to get attached," Lizzie warned. "When we know each other's names it only makes it worse in the end."

"Others?"

"You'll meet them soon when you are healed. Shouldn't be too much longer. Your back is healing nicely. The metal must have been heated perfectly. It didn't mar the rest of your flesh too much."

"Please stop," I pleaded.

"Sorry," she said. "I forget what it's like for the new girls. It's been so long."

"So long since what?"

"I went missing."

"When was that?"

She didn't answer. Instead she walked to the dirty window and picked up a glass that had been perched on the sill. It was halfway empty with an amber liquid. She drank it quickly; not throwing it back like I had seen guys do who were trying to act cool at parties. Instead, she guzzled it like she wouldn't ever get another drop again. Watching her drink the liquid reminded me that my mouth was thick from the sandwich.

"Can I have some water?" I asked. My voice trembled. I still wasn't sure where I stood with Lizzie.

Instead of water she poured me a glass of the same amber liquid and added equal amounts of cola to it. She handed it to me without ice, warm as piss. I looked at it questioningly. She answered me by handing me two pink tablets – Pepto-Bismol tablets. "New girls shouldn't drink the water. Not at first. Yasiel doesn't want you getting sick. Better to drink this anyway. Takes the edge off and makes things easier."

I sat there frozen clenching the drink and holding the tablets. Lizzie looked at me curiously. "Most of the girls that come here aren't as fresh as you. Take the drink or forget it, but you'll want it sooner or later."

She didn't say it cruelly. She said it as if she were stating a simple fact, like the world was round and water was wet. I felt as if I couldn't argue with her because I knew that she was speaking the truth.

"Where is here?"

"Nogales." She motioned for me to come to the window. I didn't move. Her face softened and she gave me a slight smile. "It's okay. Come here."

I shuffled over to her, the nightgown comforting but still aggravating my back. I wondered what had been branded on me, but I was too scared to ask and equally terrified to look.

The window overlooked a bustling city center. Not like the cities in the United States. This city scene was far more neglected and tossed to the side. Even the poorest parts of Mission Valley that I knew all too well never looked as mistreated and tired as the buildings I glimpsed packed tightly together below me. I looked to either side and saw a smattering of brightly colored houses: blue, pink, purple, green, and yellow. The houses dotted the mountainside like the colorful flowers that were planted in various areas of Mission Valley; the places that attracted the most tourists and demanded care and attention. These houses would have been just as beautiful as those flowers, yet I knew immediately they were prisons; hideaways for illicit pursuits and bouquets of violence.

"What color is this house?" I asked.

"Red," she answered as if it were the most normal question in the world.

"The color of blood," I said.

Lizzie said nothing more, but guided me away from the window, coaxed me to drink the alcoholic concoction, and sat with me until I fell asleep once again.

CHAPTER NINE

Four days after I officially became a missing girl I was moved from the blood red house to a larger house near the top of the hill. I didn't bother to notice the color. By this time I spent most of my days in a haze. Although I didn't guzzle the alcohol as greedily as Lizzie, I did nip at it frequently throughout the day. It helped lessen the pain in my back and in my heart.

Since the branding I hadn't seen Yasiel or any other men for that matter. It was just Lizzie and I and then the others when I entered the big house. When I say big house don't misunderstand me. I wasn't moved into a luxurious mansion or exquisite concubine's quarters. This house had four rooms. The kitchen had hardly any cupboards and the table had one leg shorter than the other three. The bathroom had a bathtub that was discolored with black mold creeping up the sides and no toilet, only a hole in the ground. Then there was the main room and a bedroom. The main room had sleeping bundles shoved up against the walls and bean bag chairs with their filling oozing out placed in a semi-circle around a box television. The television had those rabbit ears that I had seen on re-runs of 1980s television shows. The bedroom had a simple bed with a humble quilt that was entirely out of place in this house along with a crucifix hanging over the window. I shivered.

"Whose room is this?"

"It is for Yasiel when he . . . when he visits." Lizzie

49

seemed to choke on this last word.

"What is he? Your boyfriend?" I said it snotty because why did I have to be gracious? Why did I have to extend kindness to anyone who played a part in ripping me from my other existence?

"Of course not," she said sharply, drawing in her breath as if I had plunged a knife deep within her chest.

"I sleep there." She pointed to a bundle near the door. "We save the bed for the children."

That's when I noticed a few sad looking stuffed animals lying about the floor and children's clothing mixed in with the few clothes that hung on a makeshift laundry line across the kitchen. As if on cue, two children came running into the home with a haggard looking woman following close behind; on her hip was another child with dirty cheeks and tangled hair. I couldn't tell if it was a boy or girl.

"*¿Quién es esta chica?*" The woman spat.

"My name is Sophia," I answered with my American accent.

The woman raised an eyebrow and looked at Lizzie. "*¿Americano?*"

Lizzie nodded and the woman laughed. "Aye, this one is going to have an adjustment. Yes?"

Lizzie ignored her and so did I. "This is Marcela and these are her children: Juan, Pablo, and Lucia."

"You have to watch the children tonight. Yasiel wants me working a double." She handed the child off to Lizzie.

"Take care of yourself tonight, Marcela," Lizzie cautioned.

"Always." Marcela turned on her heel to leave and looked back at me over her shoulder. She started to say something, but changed her mind. She shook her head instead and walked out the door.

Lizzie took the toddler into the kitchen and found some crackers to keep her occupied. She told the other children they could go outside and play, but they needed to stay close to the back door. "*¿Entiendes?*" she asked.

They nodded with eyes wide and grins even wider. I

couldn't tell how old they were. Maybe, between the ages of three and six?

"Do you have children?" I asked.

She laughed. "Thank God, no."

Lizzie sat the child on the dirty linoleum and plunked a syringe off the floor that was lying nearby. The tip had blood encrusted on it from the last use. Lizzie didn't throw it away, but took it to the sink and ran it under hot water, using a paper towel to wipe it clean. She placed it in a container where other syringes were collected.

"Did you ever want children?" I asked.

She didn't answer right away, but when she did it was with a question of her own. "Do you understand what is happening here?"

How could I not? "Yes."

"Then why are you asking me questions like we are two suburban moms on a playdate?"

"I'm scared," I admitted.

"It gets better," she reminded me. Then, as if it were a peace offering, she answered my original question. "I may have wanted children someday, but I don't think I ever deserved them. It doesn't matter now. I can't have them anyway, which if you believe in blessings then it is a blessing."

"Are these children . . . well, um, who are their fathers?"

Lizzie shrugged. "Don't know. Not sure Marcela knows either. Doesn't really matter. It happens. Part of the deal."

The little girl ignored us, concentrating on the cracker in her mouth. She swished it around, spit it out, examined its mushy texture in her hand then put it back in her mouth again. I smiled at her innocence and then grimaced, knowing full well that I would never have children; at least not children that were my choice.

"What happens to them?"

"To who?" Lizzie asked as she tried to get the little girl to sip milk out of a broken sippy cup. I looked at Lucia. "Oh. Well, this is what happens to them."

Lizzie stood up and brushed off her pants. The veins in

her arms were larger than usual and I wondered if she had been using those syringes during the times that she disappeared from my sight. As if realizing I was scrutinizing the grotesque nature of her arms she grabbed a blanket and wrapped it around her gaunt body as she lowered herself into one of the bean bag chairs. The temperature was close to ninety degrees, but she cocooned herself in the blanket as if she were sitting in the middle of a snow storm. I sat down and played with Lucia's toes, taking a small amount of pleasure in her delighted laugh.

"But what about when they are grown, older?"

"They're sold."

I whipped my head around to look her squarely in the face. Was she joking? The somber expression told me she wasn't. "Sold for what?"

"Money. What else would they be sold for? Yasiel will pimp them out. Force them to sell their bodies. All the cartels do it. You can only sell a kilo of cocaine once, but women and children can be sold over and over again until they expire. These men won't give their workers birth control, but they will gladly hand them a sexually transmitted disease. Some members force their women to abort unintended pregnancies, but not Yasiel. He is perfectly content with his women getting pregnant. It ensures longevity in this business. It hasn't stopped him from taking others, though, to fill in the gaps."

"What about the boys?"

"He'll sell them, too. Some customers have no gender preference. But he may keep them out of the sex trade and use them as runners or assassins."

"And Marcela will just let this happen?" I asked unable to comprehend a mother watching her children be traded for sex; raised to be murders.

Lizzie gave a disgusted snort. "What choice does she have? What choice do any of us have?"

I couldn't argue with her. I could only silently watch her stand up, letting the blanket fall in a heap on the floor. In the recesses of my mind I hear Mama telling me to pick up my wet towels off the bathroom floor, "*I am not your maid, hija.*" Quickly, I averted my eyes from the blanket and pushed aside the memory.

She walked over to the corner of the room, pushing aside the sleeping bundles. She reached down into a hole in the flooring; her arm immersed into the floor nearly up to her elbow. She rummaged around for a moment and then stood up with gold, square packages in her hands. "You know how to use these? You have that talk with your mother?"

Reluctantly, I took the packages of condoms from her. I was seventeen years old. Of course, I knew what condoms were. I desperately wanted to shove them down her throat, kick and scream, and bolt out the door to freedom, but I knew I wouldn't stand a chance. Just because I didn't see the masked men didn't mean they weren't there. Their presence was felt everywhere in this house. Lizzie and I, as well as the children playing carefree out in the back may have appeared to be unguarded and free, but even a naive teenager knew better. Chains don't always have to be visible to hold you tightly in place.

"Some of the men will insist on them and will supply their own. These are the men that have families to protect, wives to hide their shameful deeds from. You can't disguise the fact that you're screwing around when your piss starts to burn and your wife comes down with a case of chlamydia. These *clients* are the ones you hope to get. Others, not so much. In cases like that you pray you dodge the bullet and that the chamber is empty when they shoot."

Listening to her talk made me sick to my stomach. It made me fearful of the inevitable future. So far I had avoided being violated. I may have been torn away from my family and my body scarred, but I still had a small bit of dignity left. But standing there as the packages became slick with sweat in my palms, I was reminded that dignity was something I would have to sacrifice for survival.

CHAPTER TEN

I awoke sometime in the middle of the night with a small foot lodged precariously in the small of my back just under the wound that was still healing. The foot belonged to one of Marcela's boys. I started to move away from the sleeping child, but was reminded of the times that Jesus would climb into my bed and try to snuggle with me. He had always been an affectionate child to the point of annoyance and embarrassment.

"Sophia, he loves his big sister," Mama had explained when I woke up in the morning to find Jesus curled up next to me with his thumb in his mouth and his too long hair tousled and tangled. I was nearly nine years old and Jesus just seven.

"I don't care. He still wets the bed, you know. That's gross. What if I wake up in a puddle of pee?"

Mama laughed. "I doubt that would happen, my sweet chicken."

I had rolled my eyes at my mama's ridiculous name for me. She always insisted on giving me pet names that were either farm animals or fruit. If she wasn't referring to me as a sweet chicken then I was her sweet peach or her pudding pie. Those stupid names only left me feeling sour, far from sweet. In fact, the next time that I awoke to find Jesus lying next to me I purposely pushed him out of the bed and feigned ignorance when he startled awake, rubbing his head and calling for Mama. From that night forward, I didn't have to worry about waking up in a wet bed with my little brother hogging the sheets.

Instead of pushing this boy away, I left his foot where it was and pretended that I was back in my bed at home safe and sound with Jesus sleeping next to me and Mama down the hall. Just as I was about to doze off again I heard soft voices coming from the kitchen. I kept my eyes closed, but my ears open.

"Does she know?" Marcela's heavily accented voice asked in flawless English.

"She knows enough." Lizzie answered in her American accent that sounded like mine.

"I hate the way he taunts the new girls. Makes them think the worst is behind them by making them wait so long for their first job. It's cruel."

"Preaching to the choir, Marcela. But it will come soon enough."

I heard the distinctive sound of a can being popped open. Funny how a sound can nearly send a person into a deep depression, but that popping sound again reminded me of Mama and home. If there was one thing Mama loved it was her diet soda. We always had a surplus of soda cans at our house. When Jesus and I were younger we would stack them up outside in our small backyard and pretend we were bowling, using a practically deflated basketball that was a left over Christmas gift from Mr. Debold.

"She's pretty," Marcela said. "She'll bring good business for Yasiel. It will make him happy."

"Yep," Lizzie agreed. "The happier he is the better for everyone."

There was a lull in talking. I smelled smoke curling around my nose and buried my head in the sorry excuse for a pillow to avoid coughing.

"I have a plan," Marcela announced.

"You always have a plan. We all know how those work out. Remember what happened to Elena?"

"*Elena estaba loca.* She deserved what she got."

"No one deserves what they get, Marcela."

"You really believe that? This is different anyway."

"How?"

The chair creaked as one of the women stood up. I calmed my breathing and made sure my eyes were shut, but not too tight. Tight eyes are a sure sign you are listening to a conversation not meant for your ears. I heard the door to the mini-fridge open and another can pop.

"Yasiel is planning on taking us across the border tomorrow. Well, not you. I know. You're special." Marcela said this not cruelly, but matter-of-factly.

"There's no such thing as special in hell," Lizzie retorted.

"He's rounding up me, the new girl, and a few other workers that he won in a bet that he had with another lieutenant. There's a convention in Tucson at the end of the week. Yasiel is hoping to profit from it."

"How do you know all of this?" Lizzie asked.

Marcela laughed. Her laugh was loud and raucous causing the little boy sleeping next to me to jump. It seemed he might wake up and interrupt the conversation but then he curled up into a ball and rolled away from me.

Marcela's laugh reminded me of the way Mama would laugh when she wasn't worrying about paying bills or looking for Papa. Even though he had been gone for so many years, I still heard her every once in a while talking on the phone to someone in this language that was too foreign to me to understand. I knew they were talking about Papa. After all these years she couldn't let him go and now she would have to search for me too. I wondered how many times a person could lose someone so close to them before they couldn't bear to look life in the face anymore.

This time I squeezed my eyes tight to stop the tears that were again threatening to fall from my eyes. Instead of thinking about my family, I concentrated on deciphering the thick words that Marcela spoke.

"You know those men are stupid. They think that all these drugs they give us when they are using us makes it impossible to understand what is really going on, but they are *ignorante* . . . what's the American phrase? Aw, *sí*, they are dim-witted."

"Maybe, but they're dangerous, Marcela."

"Yasiel brought me to this party at the lieutenant's house. I was supposed to entertain one or two of his suppliers. Afterwards, as the men were pulling up their pants and walking out the door I heard them discussing plans. They were arguing about whether or not it was the right time to send a group across the border. Apparently, the *gringos* are starting to pay more attention to the situation."

"What's your plan?"

"I need to get my children out of here, Lizzie. This is not a life for children. They're innocent now, but for how long? The older they get the greater the risk that they will be sold. You can't raise children in a place like this. There are people that will take my children and raise them as their own."

"How? How do you know this?"

"Some of the men . . . They talk to me. They tell me things," she said.

Lizzie snorted. "They tell you lies."

"Not some of the *gringos*. A man visited me one night a couple of weeks ago when Yasiel took us across the border to work that club. Do you remember?"

"How could I forget?"

Marcela's voice had become tense and excitable all at the same time as she began to tell her story, but the somber tone of Lizzie's dampened the urgency. Her voice softened. "He paid money for a private session with me, but he never touched me. Instead he told me he could help me. There was a way for me to keep me and my children safe. There are places across the border that will take my children."

"For money? You're selling your children for money?"

I heard what sounded like a hand hitting the table and Marcela's voice rose sharply. "I am not selling my children. I am saving them from this life of lust and despair. I would rather never see my children again and know they are living your so-called American dream than to never see them again because they are buried in a shallow grave."

"It's too risky."

"I am not stupid, Lizzie. I know that you are given special privileges because you are Yasiel's plaything, but I thought we looked out for each other. Who else do we have?"

The women didn't speak for several minutes, providing me the opportunity to hear the hum of music coming from the street down below and the gentle wheezing of the children sleeping next to me. I could even hear skittering in the walls and tried to tell myself it was simply crickets, not mice.

"You want to bring the children across the border with you?" Lizzie asked.

"We can sneak them in the van, sí?"

"No, Marcela. We cannot do that. It's not logical. Borders trips are highly organized. Yasiel would not risk loose ends. You know this."

Immediately, I heard sobbing. It was the kind of weeping that a person did when it became evident that nothing in life would ever be the same again. It was the same kind of weeping Mama was doing as she lay in bed wondering where I had gone. This kind of sobbing accompanies the realization that no matter what you do, no matter how many deals you make with yourself or with God, that you can't change the inevitable.

"I can take the boys," Lizzie finally said. "I'll go in your place and I will take the boys. I will get them safely in the hands of the man you mentioned and they will be free. You'll have to stay back to take care of Lucia in case something should go wrong."

How does a mother choose which of her children she saves, I wondered. What would Mama have said if she were given the option of losing Jesus to a bullet or me to this imprisonment? As twisted as it may seem, I am glad I didn't have to make her choose. I chose for her. In its simplest form, Lizzie was making the choice for Marcela, too. She didn't argue. She accepted that this was the only logical way to get some of her children out alive.

"*Sí, sí! Gracias dios!* But, how? Yasiel will be suspicious."

"Don't worry. I know how we can handle Yasiel, but it might hurt a bit."

To this Marcela said, "You know when I was a little girl I wanted to be a ballerina."

Lizzie sighed. "Didn't we all?"

CHAPTER ELEVEN

An unexpected strike on my right temple jolted me from what had been a short and fitful sleep. Immediately, I acted on impulse and pushed myself up against the wall, moving away from my assailant. Instead of the follow-up blow I was expecting, I felt a soft, gentle tugging on my arm and the unmistakable sound of a child's giggle. My hair had become matted to the side of my sweaty face, forcing me to awkwardly push it aside in order to determine who or what had caused my temple to begin to bleed.

It was one of the boys. What were their names again? Did it matter? After the conversation I heard last night I knew it was more important than ever to figure a way out of here. As much as I wanted to dismiss the boy, I couldn't stop staring at him as he watched me with wide eyes and an innocent smile. He was the smaller of the two, standing before me in what must have been his older brother's discarded clothing. His face was clean, but his clothes looked as if they had stains from not one but a dozen previous owners. The clothing was a joke and it was sad.

The boy pointed to the floor where I saw a book opened on its edges, forming a tent. It was an old book, one that my Mama had often read to Jesus and me. It was about a puppy that lazed his way throughout his days without a care in the world. His Mama always insisted he was poky. He was a day late and a dollar short, as Mama would say. She loved American expressions. It made her feel like she belonged, even when others preferred that she cross the border and go back home.

The boy picked up the book and offered it to me with his outstretched arms. I took it from him gingerly, as if he were handing me a grenade with a broken ring; something that could destroy me in an instant. Holding that book reminded me of my kindergarten classroom. Mrs. Lecrone's classroom was designed for small children that had big imaginations. Everything in the classroom was oversized and cozy, including a chair she kept in the reading corner. This chair was a special chair. It was bright yellow with a patchwork quilt slung over the arm and a purple heart-shaped pillow that you could lay your head on. You couldn't sit in it unless you stayed on green all week long. Friday was our class's library day. In the morning, Mrs. Lecrone would put everyone's name that stayed on green into a black magician's hat. She would chant a ridiculous string of sounds and syllables that made absolutely no sense reach in and reveal the lucky duck that got to sit in the special chair and read his or her library book.

It took nearly the entire year before my name was called. I had started to worry that I would never get to snuggle under that beautiful quilt or lay my head on the soft pillow, my friends staring at me with envy while they were confined to their desks or those vinyl nap mats. When I heard my name announced I could barely contain my excitement as I waited for library time. The anticipation was worse than waiting for Jesus to finally fall asleep on Christmas Eve so Santa could come.

Once we came back from the library, I ran straight for that chair and jumped into the middle of it, landing on my knees. When the sunlight filtered through the window, dust particles floated around me like glitter. I spent the entire twenty minutes allotted to reading time wrapped up in that blanket that smelled like musk, kicking my feet against the arm chair, watching the glittery dust dance in the air.

I was so wrapped up in my memory that I didn't notice the

boy creep closer until I felt him fold himself into my lap. He didn't say anything. He merely waited patiently, with his finger in his mouth, for me to read the book to him. I searched the room for Marcela and found her sitting silently on the floor near the door. She looked at me strangely. I couldn't tell if she was pleased that her son had wandered in my direction or if she was disgusted. Again, I remembered the conversation I had overheard before I fell asleep and decided the look on her face wasn't either of those emotions. It was sadness in its purest form.

I began to tell the story of the slovenly puppy, oblivious to what was about to occur next. About halfway through the story, Marcela approached me.

"Up," she said. I thought she was talking to the boy so I put the book down and nudged him to obey his Mama. She ignored the boy as he walked to her. Instead she repeated her command. "You. Get up!"

My feet were still asleep and wouldn't cooperate, which seemed to enrage Marcela. She reached down, grabbed me by my hair and yanked me to my feet.

"Ouch! Stop!" I shouted. This was how girls always seemed to fight – grab the hair. I had seen it a dozen times at home. There was a time when assaults between girls at my school became so often and random that I had resorted to wearing my hair up in a hat to avoid being a target.

Marcela didn't say anything as she dragged me by my hair, shoving me into a wall so hard that I would have sworn that it cracked and molded around me. After my back hit the wall she grabbed me again and threw me into one of the bean bag chairs. I narrowly missed cracking my head on the outdated television. She started to come at me again, but stopped when Lizzie came barreling at her.

The two women held onto each other as they rolled across the floor. They landed near the wall with Lizzie on top, her small fists pummeling Marcela's face. The sound of flesh on flesh was nauseating. I looked around for help and then realized that no one was paying any attention to me. This was the chance I was waiting for. I jumped up and started to run for the front door, but it was too late. The door stood wide open, my escape blocked by two men I had not seen before. Ignoring me, they ran over to break up the fight. While watching them pull the two women apart, I felt a hand on my shoulder and hot breath on my neck.

***

"Look at her face," Yasiel said. His nostrils were flaring as he stood above Lizzie, pointing at Marcela, whose face was ravaged and bleeding profusely. She sat limply against the wall looking at nothing in particular. "I had plans for her."

"Yes, I know all about your little plan. You didn't share it with me," said Lizzie.

"I don't have to share things with you. Your job is to make sure my girls are ready to perform. How am I supposed to take her across the border like this? The police are going to be all over that convention, looking out for you whores."

He shoved Lizzie hard. She tripped over a toy that belonged to one of the children and landed on her butt. She jumped up quickly, walked straight to Yasiel and slapped him across the face. One of the men standing next to Marcela raised his gun.

Instead of ordering the man to shoot, Yasiel wrapped his hand around Lizzie's throat and pushed her backwards. "That's a couple grand you cost me."

"I have a better deal for you," Lizzie said.

"I don't make deals with whores," he said.

I stood in a corner of the room watching this strange interaction. I felt certain that if I or Marcela had went after him the way Lizzie had that we would have been dead on the spot. But Lizzie seemed to have some sort of hold over him that I couldn't understand.

"This is a deal you don't want to pass up." Yasiel refused to let go of Lizzie, but he said nothing. She continued to talk. "The boys . . . There's a man that is willing to pay for them. Marcela told him no, but she's stupid. Take me with you across the border. I'll make you ten times what those other men would have paid for a go at her."

Yasiel let her go, running his hands through his hair and straightening his clothes. It was quite obvious he didn't like to get his hands dirty. "Where?"

"The Renaissance. Here." She reached into the back of her pocket and pulled out a crumbled napkin that had a writing on it, presumably a number. "This is where you can reach the man. Confirm the story for yourself. Set it up, Yasiel. I'll make it happen."

He laughed and made that same tsk-tsk sound that he had the first time I met him. "I have men to do that."

This time it was Lizzie's turn to laugh. "You have men? Men that will escort two little boys through a crowded American city to meet another man? Even you have to admit that looks suspicious. It's better if it's a woman. You're already taking a chance moving the women across the border. Why would you want to risk anything more?"

Yasiel stopped to consider this and I realized that Lizzie's breathing had slowed. Her breathe wasn't as ragged. Her words not as desperate. She seemed to have him by the balls and he knew it. He motioned to the man to lower his weapon. The older boy had emerged from wherever he had been hiding and ran towards his mother. The other man standing near her shoved him away and laughed. Her younger son sat on top of my sleeping bundle clutching his book, crying hard.

"Take them," he ordered his men. Then he turned his attention to me. As he stepped toward me fear spread like a California wildfire from the tips of my toes to my ragged split ends. Although he had been enraged seconds earlier, his smile had now returned. He took my head in his hands and kissed the center of my forehead. As gentle as this kiss was, it didn't reassure me. Then he spoke words that made it very clear what was expected of me. "Take her, too. But don't touch her. *Gringos* pay for purity."

As one of the men gathered up the screaming boys, who were reaching out to their unresponsive mother, the other man took me by the arm and led me out of the house. I looked over my shoulder one last time to see Yasiel walking towards the bedroom. "Come on, Lizzie. Let's make that deal official."

CHAPTER TWELVE

The men took me and the boys to another house at the
bottom of the hill. The boys were locked in a room with
flimsy walls that did nothing to drown out their continued fits
of rage. The men just laughed each time a small body would
fling itself against the wall, feeble attempts to free themselves
and return to their mother. I hoped that someone would hear
the commotion and come to rescue us, but I realized that this
hill with its cheerily colored houses was the lair of a tyrant
that watched over the city below, demanding that everyone
accept the wrongdoings and go about their business.
Communities like these accept the violence and the despair
because to rise against it is useless. It will only get you killed.

I was directed to another room in the house where I was
handed a brown paper bag filled with clothing. The clothes
were too tight and too revealing; a white tube top that
shimmered with glitter accents, a faded denim skirt that
barely touched the middle of my thighs, and platform shoes a
size too small that added about four inches to my height.
"No," I said when I realized that I was expected to wear these
clothes meant to show off what men wanted to buy.

The smaller of the two men walked toward me. "What did
you say?" He was missing a front tooth, causing him to speak
with a lisp. His hair was greased back with oil; his face one
big pothole from a bad case of adult acne.

"No," I said again. The man lunged at me and I jumped
back. He stumbled over his feet, falling into the door frame.
His partner laughed, enraging the tiny man even more.

"You will put those clothes on if I have to rip those off," he said, sputtering spit from his raw lips. He reached for me, but was stopped by his partner.

"*Basta ya*!" The other man yelled. "That's enough. You touch her and Yasiel will castrate you. His orders were clear."

The tiny man shrugged him off and walked away, giving me the once over before he disappeared down the hall. His partner pointed a finger at me. "Put them on if you know what is good for you."

Think, think, think, I told myself over and over again. I turned in circles looking for a way out, but there were no windows, no doors. It was a barren room with stained walls and holes in the floor. Just then the door opened and Lizzie walked in. Her hair was disheveled, her shirt was on inside out, and she walked tenderly across the floor. I shuddered, imaging what had happened once the boys and I were removed. She sat down slowly on the floor, wincing as she tried to get comfortable.

"What happened?" I asked her.

"You ask too many questions," was her response. She refused to look at me.

"Why did you do that?"

"Do what? Beat her?" Her voice was muffled. She sat with her knees up, her head on her knees and her arms outstretched in front of her. That's when I noticed the marks that were not there earlier in the evening; three red, circular burn marks that dotted the top of her hands. Then I recalled that Yasiel had lit a cigarette when he demanded that she follow him to that sparse bedroom. I cringed, thinking about where else he may have extinguished his fury. "It was necessary."

I turned my attention away from the wounds and decided to try another approach. "I know about your plan."

This evoked a response. She looked up sharply. "I don't know what you are talking about."

"Yes, you do. You and Marcela were talking last night."

"Stop right now," she said. "The less you know the

better."

"Yasiel will kill you."

"No, he won't. Rape me? Yes. Torture me? Yes. But he will not kill me. He's in my debt."

"For what?" I couldn't possibly imagine how a man like him would be in anyone's debt, much less a woman's.

She answered by absentmindedly rubbing the scar on her neck. "You need to forget what you heard."

"Help me," I whispered.

"What?"

"Help me. Get me out of here."

Lizzie shook her head. "I can't."

"You said you would protect me."

Lizzie shook her head and looked away from me. "I knew better than to tell you that. How? How can I protect you if you refuse to listen to me? Do what you're told. Keep your head down and stay out of business that you know nothing about. That is how I can protect you."

"Fine," I said moving away from her. "I'll help myself."

"Girls that talk like that end up disappearing."

"I've already disappeared."

"It's worse to disappear from here. At least here you are alive."

"This isn't a life."

"Beats the alternative."

I ignored her, turned my back to her, and changed into the offensive clothes. "You must have had a pathetic life before if you think this is living. Did you not have a family? People that cared about you? Don't you want to see them again?"

"Yes, I have family. But seeing them again, now, after all I have been through and everything I have done would be unbearable. You'll learn soon enough that in order for a victim to survive they have to think like their captors. I am ashamed of the things I have done to survive a mere two flights above hell."

Before putting the shoes on I turned to her, taking a moment to study her. It dawned on me that she was like me.

She was someone's daughter; maybe someone's sister or aunt. As detached as she pretended to be, at one point she was exactly like me. "Tell me about your family."

"No," she said.

"Why?"

"Because what does it matter?"

I sat down beside her, realizing just how quickly life had shifted. Days ago I had been a bratty teenager feeling sorry for myself because I had to spend an evening doing chores to help out my mama. Now, the feelings that swelled in my heart and threatened to send an embolism to my brain were causing me to seek comfort from this woman who clearly wanted to keep me at an arm's length. Sitting beside her, I knew that I would never again experience a relationship with another human being that wasn't tainted. I knew what my captors had in store for me. I knew that even if I was able to figure out a way to break free and find my way back home that I wouldn't be whole again. I was broken like the woman sitting next to me and for one moment I wanted to feel connected to another person. An overwhelming desire filled me, not a physical desire but the type of emotional longing to share a moment with another person; to hold a secret between the two of you even if the moment is fleeting and ultimately meaningless.

Perhaps she read my mind or had a moment of weakness, because she turned to me and held my gaze. She pushed a strand of my hair behind my ear and shook her head. The tough exterior crumbled for a few moments as she smiled and her eyes glistened. "You remind me so much of her."

"Who?" I asked.

"My sister."

"What's her name?"

"Emily. She was always a fighter. Our mother said she was born kicking and screaming. She refused to let someone tell her they couldn't be saved. She never gave up on me. Funny how twins can be so different."

"Twins? Do you look alike?" It was a childish question,

but I couldn't think of anything else to say and I didn't want her to stop talking.

Again she put her hand to her neck, rubbing the jagged scar then examining her marred arms. "Not anymore."

"Where is she now?"

She shrugged. "I wouldn't know. It's been a long time. For all I know she is dead. I don't feel her like I used to, but then again you learn to stop feeling after a while. You'll see what I mean."

She turned away from me and that's when I noticed the black cross at the base of her throat. "Was that hers?" I asked.

She touched the cross and shook her head. "No. This belonged to someone else."

"Someone special?"

She took a moment to answer then said flatly, "No."

"So why do you wear it?"

She looked at me again this time with fire in her eyes. "I wear it to remind me that God can't save you. You can only save yourself."

CHAPTER THIRTEEN

This is how it went down. Just before the sun rose the boys and I, along with Lizzie, were escorted into the back of a non-descript white truck with Arizona license plates. We were tossed into the back of the truck, wedged between boxes of nectarines, avocados, and honeydew. The boys sat next to Lizzie sniffling and trembling. Before we left the house and loaded into the van, Lizzie warned me not to comfort or say anything to the boys.

"It has to be this way," she insisted. "They have to believe they are being abandoned."

"Why?" I asked.

Again, she looked at me like I was a stupid, naive girl. I guess I was. "Because it will foil the plan. They won't understand. Besides it is better that they hate her."

"What kid wants to hate their parent?"

"If they hate her they will never come looking for her. They will have the life that she sacrificed so much for them to have."

"What about Lucia?"

Lizzie frowned. "I don't know. We'll do what we can for her, but I don't know if I can pull this off again. I am risking so much as it is."

"You are these boys' savior," I said.

"You're wrong. I am nobody's savior."

The truck rambled along the road for about an hour and a half, tossing us into the boxes of fruit and into each other. I didn't realize until I heard the men in the front of the truck speaking to the border patrol that Nogales was so close to the

United States border. It gave me hope. Maybe I could find a way back across the border after tonight. Maybe I could find my way back to my family. But then I looked at Lizzie, who had her eyes averted from me, and I realized that maybe it wasn't that easy. Being so close to the U.S. border wasn't a fine line between deliverance and desperation, but a treacherous valley.

The entire trip into Tucson took under an hour and a half. We were shoved out of the truck into an alley. The passenger of the truck handed Lizzie a piece of paper, a prepaid cellphone, and a couple of American bills.

"Room numbers for both buyers are written here. You are to take the girl with you to meet the buyer for the boys, then deliver her to this room." He stabbed his stubby finger at the writing on the paper. "*El Jefe* says to call him when the deal is done. We will pick you up here afterwards."

Lizzie nodded and tucked the piece of paper into her back pocket, the bills in her bra, and held onto the phone.

"Buyers?" I asked. She didn't answer. She merely gave me a solemn look and I understood; the buyer for the boys and the buyer for me.

"*Vámonos!*" Lizzie said to the boys roughly. They refused to move, standing between us and the man, looking down at their feet. The man moved forward towards the boys, but Lizzie put up a hand. She turned to me, jerking her head towards the small figures standing helpless and alone. I took their small, smooth hands to lead them away. Lizzie turned to follow, but was stopped by the man. He held her to him by her arm. He put his nose up against hers and although I was a good ten feet away, I could smell his stale cigarette breath as he delivered a message.

"Don't mess this up. *El Jefe* hasn't been too pleased with you lately. This goes bad and you may find yourself falling out of favor with the boss. You know what happens to people that cross Yasiel, right? It don't matter if you're his whore. And, you-" he said, pointing to me. "Don't get any ideas and think this is a field trip. You run. We find you. Then we find your family." With that the man cackled and shoved Lizzie away from him. He ran alongside the truck to the passenger's side and the truck sped away, spewing exhaust.

She didn't say anything as we walked side by side through the dark alley. A couple of kids about my age, maybe a little younger, were standing in front of a brick wall drinking tall cans of beer and adding brightly colored, bold illustrative touches to the wall. They paid little attention to us, not worried about being caught or just simply not carrying one bit if they were. I envied their juvenile delinquency because it meant they were free to be stupid kids.

We turned the corner, blending quickly in with the crowd. It was a warm night, but it didn't stop people from going about their business. There were several restaurants with outdoor patios, hosting patrons who were laughing, drinking, and enjoying life. People were walking their dogs. Others were standing in line at a two screen theater. Did any of them look at us? Did any of them consider the fact that we looked out of place? Certainly someone ought to notice that a skimpily dressed teenager holding the hands of two little boys wasn't ordinary. Or was it? Were people immune to suffering? Did they notice, but refuse to accept that such anguish could actually be front and center, interrupting their dinner, interfering with their movie plans?

I considered running. What could anyone do about it? Gun me down on a crowded street? I already feared my days were numbered, but just as quickly, I remembered that running would have repercussions. It would cost me more than I was willing to pay. If I tried to escape right here, in this moment, without a plan Jesus and Mama would become causalities of my recklessness. They would be hunted them down. They would be tortured and murdered. I knew this in my heart. Did I want this life? No. But I was willing to accept my fate if it meant that they would be spared. It was the last gift I would ever give them.

The Renaissance Hotel was not nearly as glamorous as its name alluded to. Instead, it was a two story dump that seemed less like a hotel and more like a homeless shelter. Aside from the unsavory crowd loitering around the front steps, the lobby had that vagrant smell; a booze and body odor type of cologne. Behind a layer of shatterproof glass, a plump man with thinning hair and a swollen nose balanced on a stool in a cubicle that was too small for his large frame. Behind him a red, 19-inch television was tuned to one of those 24 hour news stations. The man didn't look like he was one to care much about what the news had to say. In fact, he seemed to be disinterested in anything around him. He didn't even seem to notice us until Lizzie rapped on the glass.

Words were not exchanged, but a couple of bills switched hands. I figured it was the hotel's reimbursement for letting their property be the scene of wickedness and sinful behavior. We stepped into an elevator that smelled worse than the lobby. It reeked of stale urine and the floor was coated with something sticky. I thought I might be sick, but the younger boy beat me to it when he leaned forward and vomited on the floor. His older brother patted his back and wrapped a comforting arm around him. I looked at Lizzie, but she stared straight ahead. Is this how she managed? Did she mentally go somewhere else to avoid the pain and hopelessness of these situations? Would I someday lose my ability to empathize and comfort, too?

Room 222 was at the end of a narrow hall. Most of the wall sconces were broken, providing very little light and intensifying the menacing atmosphere. I reached out to put my hand on the older boy's shoulder and he shrugged me off. He scowled at me with intense abhorrence. Those small, childish eyes looked older beyond their years and seemed to suggest that I was responsible for everything that had happened to him from the moment he burst forth between his mother's legs into this world to that very moment. I wanted to reassure him. Let him know about the life that lay ahead of him, but suddenly I was doubtful.

How did we know the man on the other side of the door in room 222 was the rescuer Marcela claimed? What if he had lied to her to simply get his hands on two children to use as he pleased? Worse than that, what if Lizzie was wrong? What if these two children grew up to discover the truth and decided to return to Mexico to search for their mother and sister? Would they find nothing but a cold, unmarked grave that contained their remains? There were so many questions, but the ultimate question was why I cared. These boys, their mother, this stoic woman walking in front of us – what did they matter to me? I should have been worried about myself, but instead I was worried about these strangers like they were family. It didn't make sense, but in the same breath it did. They were my family now – a family of circumstance.

The man in room 222 opened the door immediately. When I saw him my heart tightened. What had I expected? Maybe I thought these children's rescuer would be a hard-edged, brusque man; someone like Bruce Willis or Vin Diesel, or that guy from those boxing movies. What was his name? But the man that opened the door and ushered us briskly into the dim room was nothing at all like those action stars. Instead, he wore tiny wire-rimmed glasses, had a comb-over and peach fuzz for a mustache. He was tiny in both height and width. He wore a red button-down shirt tucked into a pair of Wrangler jeans without a belt and vivid white tennis shoes. *Did he buy these just for this meeting*, I thought.

He was nervous. He stood in front of us wringing his hands then running his fingers through his hair, messing up his comb-over style. He cleared his throat about five times before speaking.

"I was expecting the mother."

"Too dangerous," Lizzie stated.

"Yes, yes, I understand. Okay, so, um, so let the mother know that her boys will be safe. We will get them new identities. We'll take care of them." He smiled awkwardly at Lizzie and I then looked at the boys. After a long moment, he turned away and reached for an envelope that sat atop the nightstand. He handed it to Lizzie. She took it and peered inside.

"What's this?"

The man's nervous fidgeting began again. "Um . . . well, the man that arranged this meeting was very clear that a monetary exchange would need to happen. He instructed me to give you the amount that is in the envelope. The agency I work for is willing to pay."

Lizzie tossed the envelope onto the bed. "I'm not selling these children to you. That is not the nature of this arrangement."

"I understand that. It was not the arrangement I had with the mother either and quite honestly I wasn't prepared to make a deal with your –" He struggled to find the right word. "With your boss, but the last thing our agency wants is for you to face the consequences if you do not return with some form of payment. Take the money and be smart. We know the risk you took bringing the children to us."

Lizzie retrieved the envelope from the bed and counted the bills. She handed the envelope to the man. "I told you I won't sell you these children. I am fully aware of the consequences. Maybe I don't care. Use the money to buy them clothes, food, some real toys. Make them feel safe, happy, and loved. Give them things money can't buy. But if I ever find out that this so-called "agency" isn't what you told the mother it is then you should worry about the consequences."

The man nodded. "You don't have to worry. We won't hurt the children. No one will hurt these children. We will place them in a loving home. They'll grow up well and loved," he assured us.

Lizzie seemed satisfied with that answer. She turned away from the anxious man and motioned for me to walk out the door. When I tried to say something to the boys she gently put her hand on my shoulder and shook her head. "It has to be this way. Soon they will forget. They will think their life here with us and their mother was a bad dream they are grateful to have woken up from."

***

The next room listed on the sheet of paper in Lizzie's back pocket was 303. Instead of riding the elevator we took the stairs. Lizzie moved slowly, calculating each step. She kept me ahead of her, presumably to keep me from running away. While she may have been willing to sacrifice herself for Marcela's children, I wasn't under any false impressions that she would do the same for me. I was always within an arm's length of her reach. But when we reached the top of the stairs she stopped me. For the first time she said my name.

"Sophia."

It sounded unnatural to hear my name spoken. Back home my name fell from my mama's tongue in a variation of forms depending on the nature of her calling to me; sternly, attaching my middle name when I had pissed her off; melodically, when she would sit on the couch, patting the cushion next to her, and ask me to join her to tell her about my day. Friends and teachers muttered the three syllables that completed my name without giving a second thought to what it would be like if you were nameless and unable to be identified by a set of syllables that bounced off the tongue. I hadn't heard a single soul mutter my name in days. Not since right before Yasiel ordered his men to emblazon their mark on my back. Up until that moment, I never realized how special a name was. It was more than something that identified you to strangers; a name meant you were connected. You were linked to the people around you. It made you tangible, noticeable; a part of the universe – a being that couldn't simply be expunged from a person's mind.

"Sophia, listen to me." Her voice wavered. "You asked me to deliver you from this hell. I wish I could. Maybe someday I can."

She paused, looking me directly in the eyes. The words that tumbled from her lips sounded like the words of a coach giving their player sage advice for how to play the game. Only in this game the prize wasn't a plastic trophy or a blue ribbon, it was an extension of my life. It didn't matter that my existence would irretrievably change when I stepped across the threshold of room 303. What mattered was that I knew how to strategically play the game this night so I would continue to breathe, even if I wasn't sure it was worth it.

"I understand," I said.

Lizzie put her hand on my shoulder. Her fingertips were ice cold. "I don't think you do. We have to stick together. We have to be loyal to each other, otherwise we lose our souls. Yasiel and these men behind these doors may take our bodies. They may try to extract every last shred of moral dignity we have, but we control our souls. Thank you for helping me tonight. You took a risk by not telling Yasiel what you knew. So while I can't ultimately rescue you, I can repay you."

I frowned. "How?"

She smiled at me, warmly and lovingly. "Stay here. Don't make a sound. Don't run. You won't get far if you do. Other girls have tried and it has ended badly. There are eyes everywhere. Of course, if you make the decision to leave I won't begrudge you of that choice. I would understand. "

She turned away from me and opened the door to the hallway. That's when I understood. She was repaying me for my loyalty. She was in my debt for my silence. The currency was my innocence.

"I'll be back soon, Sophia."

CHAPTER FOURTEEN

I sat in the stairwell leaning against the cool cinder block wall for over an hour. I covered my ears trying to drown out the sound of the voices in my head telling me to run, to get away. I wanted to. I was on United States soil. How hard could it be to defy Lizzie's orders to stay? But then I realized that I was a prisoner on United States soil. I wasn't free to walk out of this hotel, to find the nearest police cruiser and beg the officer to take me home to Mama. Who would believe me? To them I would be just another runaway teen, a whore, or a crack head; someone that would be tossed aside and left to fend for myself. I would be in the line of fire, the clichéd sitting duck. If I stayed put and didn't run, maybe there would be a chance in the future. Maybe Lizzie could make it happen. We could cross the border together and find our families. I could touch, smell, and feel Mama and Jesus again. She could find peace with her sister. Did I really believe all this nonsense? I must have because why didn't I run?

When Lizzie reappeared in the stairwell her eyes were blacker than usual. She refused to look me. At first I thought she was angry with me for allowing her to sacrifice herself, but then I realized it was shame. It's funny how prisoners feel shame for something they ultimately have no control over. Not comical, but unsettling. You may think she had a choice. You may think that I had a choice, but no one has a choice when they can be bought and sold like cattle.

"We have to make this believable." With that she ripped the strap of my tank top. The material separated without resistance, as if it understood it had no choice either. I put my hand to my chest to hold the shirt in place. Next, she ruffled my hair. "That's good. Let's go."

She started to walk down the steps, but I stopped her by gently grabbing her wrist. "Thank you."

She acknowledged my thank you with a slight nod then pulled her wrist free from my soft grip and walked down the steps. We didn't speak as we retraced our steps from earlier in the evening. There was still a gregarious crowd of people filling their stomachs with food, guzzling drinks, and taking full advantage of their sovereignty without paying one bit of attention to two broken people. Teenagers tend to walk through their lives hoping to remain anonymous, blending in with their peers, making certain that they don't stand out. *Be careful what you wish for*, Mama had always said.

What had I wished for? Sometimes I wished that Mama would leave me alone and quit quizzing me about my day. It was high school after all. The days were monotonous, just like her questions. I wished Jesus would quit barging in on me when I was trying to get ready in the mornings or that he wouldn't loiter in the hallway and living room when Hayden came over. I knew he had a crush on her and it irked me. Yes, be careful what you wish for because when your wishes are finally granted they rarely take the form you imagined.

When we reached the alley the white truck was waiting for us, as well as a black sedan with impenetrable tinted windows. The teenagers that had been adding their street art to the wall were gone. A scrappy looking dog was nosing around a dumpster. It started to run to us then seemed to think better of it and quickly ran the other way. As we approached the white truck, the man from earlier jumped out of the passenger's side, then Yasiel emerged from the sedan. He motioned for Lizzie to hand him the money and the cell phone. She handed him the cell phone first, which he promptly tossed to the side and stepped on. It was just another thing in his operation that was expendable.

Next, she handed him the money. The other man took me by the elbow and started to lead me away. "Wait," Yasiel said.

We stopped. I observed Yasiel counting the money. "Where's the rest?"

Lizzie shrugged. "That's it."

"That's it." He repeated. "Not according to my calculations. You promised me a big payday, Lizzie."

She put her hands in her back pockets, briefly meeting my eyes. Then she raised her palms to the sky. "I don't know what to tell you. He wouldn't pay. What was I supposed to do?"

"I see," Yasiel said. He walked around Lizzie in a circle, once, twice, three times. All the while he counted the money over and over again.

"This is pretty shitty, Lizzie. I thought we had a deal?"

Again she briefly caught my eyes, and then looked away. "You know how these things go. I'm sure you have ways of getting your money back. You're resourceful."

I watched their game of cat and mouse, feeling the hairs on my arms starting to rise. She was taunting him. Did she want him to kill her? I couldn't be sure, but I was pretty certain she would welcome death. It seemed like the fight had leaked out of her. She was simply passing the time until she could anger him enough that he would be tired of being obligated to her for something I didn't understand.

Yasiel stopped in front of her. "Yes, yes. But then again, so are you. I should have known better. My mistake, Lizzie."

He reached into his suit pocket, withdrawing a pocket knife. He flicked it open. Its serrated edge reflected light from one of the few street lights in the alley. He inserted the blade into Lizzie's hair, slowly twisted her hair with the blade. She didn't move. She kept her eyes locked on his, daring him and begging him to get it over with once and for all.

"Yes, my mistake, but it won't happen again. Will it?" He pulled the blade from her tresses then turned away from her.

It happened instantly. I had no time to reconcile what was happening. One moment I was watching Lizzie hand her life over to this monster and the next that serrated blade found its way into my stomach. I didn't feel pain. I felt release as I fell to the ground. Sounds were muted as my senses dulled. I heard Lizzie screaming, repeating the word no over and over and over again. Someone grabbed me from underneath my arms and dragged me into the back of the truck.

My eyes were open and there was darkness. No blinding, white light to warm me like Mama had always said happened when people died and their souls were released to the heavenly Father. So for a second I thought I had a chance. Even as I lay dying I still held onto some sort of hope.

I started to close my eyes because I was so tired. But that is when I heard her voice.

"Sophia, stay awake. I'm so sorry. Please, please, please, stay awake."

I started coughing and tasted metal in my mouth. It took me a moment to realize it was blood. Lizzie placed one hand under my head and used the other hand to cover my wound. Because I was lying down and the truck was so dark, I couldn't see how badly I was injured but I could feel the slickness on my skin and knew that I was bleeding profusely. I understood that it wouldn't be long.

I coughed again and started to speak.

Lizzie shook her head. She was crying. "No. Don't say anything."

I reached up to touch her. My hand caught on the black cross she wore. My fingers were entangled for only a moment and when I lowered my hand because I was too weak to sustain the effort, the necklace broke free from her. Again, she said, "I'm sorry."

It became harder to breathe. There was so much I wanted to say because I knew that I was dying. Death was working its way up my body. First, it numbed my feet, then my legs, next my bleeding wound, and soon it would find my heart. What should my last words be? They should be memorable, I thought. Before the numbness reached my heart, I managed six words, "My name is Sophia Lucia Cruz."

Want to Read More from Piper Punches?

Turn the Page for Exclusive Sneak Peaks of:

60 Days
(Coming Soon 2014)

The Waiting Room
(Released October 2013)

60 Days

"Bless me, Father. It has been twenty one years, ten hours, and twenty minutes – give or take – since my last confession." Her voice was barely audible, no more than a whisper yet the man on the other side of the sliding confessional screen seemed to have no difficulties understanding her.

He answered back in a haggard voice that was as full-bodied as a vintage bottle of wine; a hint of weariness, a touch of passion, and a rather large amount of dread. *Yes*, she thought, *he should fear what is on the other side of this screen*. But she had to approach her task with patience and serenity. The devil works in mysterious ways. She didn't want to goad him just yet. So, instead she let the priest talk.

"God welcomes your confession now, child," the voice assured her.

"Does He?" she asked as she put a hand to her throat. Her fingers rhythmically caressed the black cross that rested in the hollow of her throat. The cross had been a gift, but it had carried a curse that followed her around for twenty one years, ten hours, and twenty minutes – give or take. Today she would finally be rid of that torment if everything fell into place.

"Of course, the Lord wants to absolve you of your sins. Speak freely."

"That may not be best. Speaking freely can cause the tongue to drip venom, spreading pain and misfortune, Father." How long had it been since she had spoken to another person and called them Father; a word that signified an intimate, nurturing, and loving relationship? Twenty one years, ten hours, and twenty minutes?

She and the priest sat in silence for a long moment as she reached around her neck and released the black cross. The relief that spread through her body was climatic. The noose that had throttled her for most of her life had finally released its grip. She held the cross in her hand. It was time to conjure the devil. She wouldn't hesitate any longer. It was time to go in for the kill. Take no prisoners. Leave no wounded.

She raised her voice and spoke in a language that was familiar, yet distinctly foreign. "*¿Cuales son tu pecados, Padre?*"

The priest didn't speak, but she could hear him shift in his seat. Although the nature of the confessional screen made it difficult to discern features, she caught a slight gesture that indicated he was wiping his brow. She had caught his attention, but he hadn't answered her question.

"*¿Entiendes?*" she asked. "Do you understand? What are your sins?"

When he spoke the full-bodied tone of his voice had weakened considerably; watered down by fear and uncertainty. "I understand.   What can I do for you, child?"

"Why do you call me child?" she asked; inciting and provoking a reaction. She heard movement in the vestibule of the church, but continued with her mission. She wasn't going to let a midnight confession be disrupted by a parishioner lighting a candle for their wayward son or missing daughter.

"You are a child of the Lord."

"Do you recognize my voice, Father? You must. You must know who I am. You must know that you can't hide behind your collar and your confessional screen any longer. *Reconocerme!*" she banged her hand open-palmed against the screen displaying the black cross.

"*Aye, mi dios.*"

The words of recognition were drowned out by the rapid firing of semi-automatic weapons, exploding and echoing in the church like marbles falling from the ceiling and bouncing off the walls and the floor. She put her hands over her head and sheltered in place. Wood shrapnel from the confessional imbedded itself into her back, her arms, and her torso. She tasted blood and smelled gun powder. When the firing had ceased for several minutes, she gathered the courage to push open the confessional door amazed that she had survived the onslaught. She couldn't have known when she opened the door that her plans had been thwarted, sabotaged. She wouldn't have believed that from that night forward she would pray day and night for death to take her quickly and mercifully. *Bless me, Father, for I have sinned.*

Girls cross the border into Mexico every day and disappear. Some are missed, most are forgotten. Two months ago Emily Vega's sister, Lizzie, went in search of a mystery across the Mexican border and never returned. Another missing girl is what the Mexican authorities told her. Emily won't accept this. Letting go of her sister is not an option, but time is running out and Emily has a secret of her own.

Coming Soon
2014

Missing Girl

Chapter 1 – Charlotte
Present Day

I had never felt so many emotions in one day. Never had I found myself sobbing guttural, disgusting sobs one minute and feeling completely elated and awestruck the next. All day long I received strangers, childhood friends, even a random news crew at my mother's home; all of them offering condolences, adding their memories to the collection of things I didn't know about my mom, and telling me what a wonderful woman Dr. Sylvie Day had been. I listened politely and nodded accordingly, feeling at ease, yet utterly bewildered that my mother had touched the lives of hundreds of people in this small town, not to mention scores of others who mailed or posted social media condolences.

Each person that stepped over the threshold of my mother's two-bedroom farmhouse brought with them a symbol of their generation. The oldest of my mother's patients brought baked goods. Middle-aged women and men brought flowers or plants. The youngest visitors were teenagers, with empty hands and sullen faces, being dragged to the visitation as evidence of all the good my mother had done in this small town. After all, she had birthed at least three-fourths of them.

Of course I realized my mother was special. What child doesn't? But I didn't realize the impact that one woman could have on an entire community. When I met with Gary Reinhold of Reinhold and Sons Funeral Home to plan the services, he alluded to her impact. He sat behind a massive pine desk that flagrantly overpowered his tiny five foot six frame – a wisp of a man that had helped countless generations lay to rest their loved ones. I wondered if he ever contemplated his own demise when he was surrounded by death all the time.

"Charlotte, I am not sure we can handle the amount of visitors who will want to pay respect to your mother. God rest her soul." The funeral home was non-denominational, but Gary crossed himself, and then wiped a tear from his eye.

"Surely you have had large services before. I don't know where else to go."

Gary nodded. "Yes, yes. Well we will certainly take very good care of Sylvie and her interment, but might I make a suggestion?"

The suggestion had been to rent a massive tent, one of those used for joyous outdoor gatherings like weddings and graduations. It would be placed on my mother's property; 250 acres of farmland smack in the middle of rural Missouri – an area spacious enough to receive, welcome, and provide parking for the multitude of guests that Gary was sure would be arriving to pay their final respects.

It felt strange that a town that had a population large enough to support a Home Depot, a Walmart, and a proposed 70 million dollar outlet mall on recently sold farmland could not support more than one funeral home. I told Gary this and he shrugged sadly. "Marion is a transitory town now. People, they come and they go, staying for a short time until better things pull them away. You understand the pull. How long have you been away?" I nodded because I couldn't argue with truth. "Your mom is an icon in this town. People are going to show up for her funeral. They'll come from all over. Just you wait and see."

I was hesitant about the unconventional funeral arrangements, but my husband Nick seemed to think it made perfect sense. Taking my hand as we left the funeral home to go back to mom's farmhouse to prepare, he said, "Charlie, it makes perfect sense. Your mom wouldn't want to be laid out in a cheaply decorated funeral home. She'd want to be in a place that meant something to her. It is a perfect solution; better than St. Roberts, even."

I felt a giggle tickle my throat and I smiled. Gary had mentioned St. Roberts Cathedral as another option for the service. It had undergone a massive renovation a decade or so ago and was a modern, Roman Catholic Church that could possibly rival the size of the Sistine Chapel. "If I choose St. Roberts my mother would haunt me for the rest of my days."

Mom was a self-proclaimed agnostic. When I was little, it was a blessing because it meant I didn't have to get up early for church on Sunday mornings and listen to a ninety-year-old priest lecture about hell and damnation. Of course, I didn't know first-hand this was what happened at church. It was second hand knowledge passed along to me by Jia Lin, my best friend, who tended to overdramatize most events.

"You're so lucky," Jia would gush when she came to my house on Sunday afternoons to play with dolls or listen to Top 40 radio. "I wish my mom worked all the time so we could skip church. Boring," she said as she melodramatically rolled her eyes.

In a town as small as Marion there weren't too many people that didn't take a pause on Sunday morning to attend services. Most of Marion believed that Mom didn't attend services because she was too busy delivering God's little miracles into the world. Not because she wasn't sure God existed. My mom, a woman who never held back her opinions, was perfectly content to let people believe what they wanted. This puzzled me. Why would she lie?

"Oh, Charlotte, I have my reasons for not being sure about God. If I let other people know I felt that way, they would just try to convince me otherwise. I don't need to be convinced, guided, or shown the light. Let people think what they want and all will be fine with the world."

"Don't you think the babies you help deliver are miracles from a greater power?" I asked.

Mom smiled up at me (by then I was thirteen and at least three inches taller than her). "I certainly think you're a miracle."

I smiled at that memory as Nick opened the car door for me.

***

Gary was right. People began showing up first thing at nine the next morning. I had just finished washing out my coffee cup at the kitchen sink when I looked up and saw the line of cars beginning to snake along the property. The farmhouse sat right in the middle of the property, which meant you had to drive along a dirt road for several minutes before you made it to the house. It seemed so remote for 21st century living, but Mom loved it.

"Privacy," she always said. "These days no one takes privacy seriously, but I do. This is my retreat. I don't want to make it easy for people to intrude on us."

The trail of cars was impressive. It reminded me of the scene in Field of Dreams when visitors are being drawn to the ball field that Kevin Costner's character built. If you build it they will come. Gary had been right; there is no way that his funeral home could have handled this crowd.

Nick came up behind me, putting his strong hands on my shoulders. In that moment, I loved him more than ever. Just his presence was enough to calm me. He whistled slowly. "Wow. I hope we have enough food." We both turned to look at the measly cheese and meat spread that sat on the island waiting to be taken outside.

It turned out that it didn't matter. Everyone who embarked upon the farmhouse and gathered outside under the tent brought food – tons of food. So much food that the deep freeze Mom had in the basement couldn't accommodate it all. As I packed away the last casserole that would fit, I wondered if we'd be able to find a shelter to take the excess without offending anyone.

The stream of visitors persisted all day, the line of traffic never ceasing. There was never a lull. Never a chance to stop, catch a breath, and regroup. Receiving hundreds of guests was exhausting. There wasn't even time to retreat to the bathroom to search for Tylenol or something else to dull the headache that had begun to keep a steady beat near my right temple. I couldn't imagine what it would have been like if the visitation had been at the funeral home; standing in one place, the line never ending. At least doing it this way (because it had to be done, there was no one else that this sad, sullen task could fall to) Nick and I were able to mingle, move, and occasionally sit.

At one point early in day I caught sight of mom's casket resting underneath the gargantuan tent adjacent to the farmhouse, surrounded by a mob of people. Yet the scene was terribly lonely. I knew she was there, but she really wasn't. Tears assembled behind my eyes as I remembered the only time that my mom had wanted to host a party on this land. This was her sanctuary. She rarely even entertained close friends at the house. The only time she had offered up her privacy was when Nick and I had announced our engagement.

"Why not have your wedding here?" she had asked.

"Here?" I responded, incredulously. We had been sitting on the front porch, sipping tea out of tea cups that were someday meant to be handed down to me – china with a pink and white rosette print that was way too dainty for my urbanized tastes. It was a rare autumn day when the temperatures soared into the upper 80s. I laughed. "Why here? Do you know how many people would be trampling through the yard, mistreating your rose bushes?"

"It's a big space. You could have the wedding of your dreams," she debated. "I mean look, Charlotte. Look how much land to host a grand party for all of your friends and Nick's friends, his family." My mother gestured to the rolling fields of green that had begun to turn brown as the season progressed without a drop of rain. I couldn't bring myself to tell her that I had always been aware of how incredibly large the property was. I couldn't find a non-hurtful way of saying that I had felt trapped by its vastness for so many years, sitting in the two bedroom farmhouse unable to escape; it was an island that was surrounded by green fields of soy beans, corn, and redundancy.

"You would save so much money. To rent a space this big in Chicago would cost a fortune and you wouldn't have the scenery," she continued.

I shook my head. "Nick and I don't need a big space. He has a small family, too. Besides we weren't considering a wedding in the city anyway. We are thinking a sunset wedding in Aruba on the beach."

Mom sighed and nodded. One of her greatest qualities was not enforcing her will, although I must admit there were times when one could mistake this for not caring enough. "Yes, yes; you and your beach. You have always been drawn to the water. I understand. I just thought that by getting married here your father would, in a way, be there too."

I remembered taking mom's hands; they had begun to feel old; ropey and veiny. "He is, Mom. Right here." I brought her hands to my heart and we shared a smile.

***

"Oh, and your momma and I laughed so hard we damned near peed our knickers." Mabel Schulte cackled and squeezed my leg as she reminisced about the time that she and my mom had discovered Mabel's brother, Harold, sitting ten feet below the ground in slush and human waste. "We done told Mr. Smarty Pants that the outhouse was in bad shape, but he wouldn't listen to nothin' your Momma and I told him. Born two minutes ahead of me and he thought he always knew better. I tell you. Sylvie swore that from that day he was transformed. The waste acted like a potion that turned him into the sour nutter that he is today."

Mabel looked across the way, squinting in the sunlight. I followed her gaze and saw Harold standing alone by the growing assortment of food under a second tent that had just been brought in to shield the mounting number of mourners from the midday sun. "I take it your brother isn't the friendly type, huh?"

Mabel shrugged. After 78 years there isn't much you can

say to defend someone who had continued to disappoint and alienate people, even if that person is your own flesh and blood. "My brother didn't need to fall in a vat of shit to repel people. He seemed to have an aura of stink around him from the time he was a boy. But, aside from his Isabel, I reckon he always held a soft spot for your Momma."

I raised my eyebrows at this statement. "That's a curious thought. The only memory I have of my mom interacting with him is when she stood on that front porch with my Granddad's rifle, telling him to get off her land."

Mabel giggled and placed her hand atop my own, patting lightly; the liver spots sprinkled across the tops like confetti. "Life is complicated, you know. I suppose death brings the peace. I sure did love your momma so, even as we drifted apart over the years."

We sat there like that for some time; me contemplating whether or not death was peaceful even during times when it occurred so violently. What was Mabel thinking? I couldn't know. I could only guess that she may have been contemplating her own rapidly approaching mortality.

***

It's hard for me to imagine having any other mother than my mom. From the time I was little I knew she was special. It wasn't the way that she sang her own rendition of classic lullabies to lull me back to sleep after a fierce Midwest thunderstorm. It wasn't the way that she comforted me when Bobby Cullins called me "the turd-faced daughter of a Negro lover" when mom came to the aid of a young African-American woman who had been left to fend for herself, alone and pregnant. It wasn't the way that mom looked after me that made me realize the depth of her worth not only as a mother, but a human being. No, it was the way that she looked after the women that lived, breathed, and sometimes died in Marion.

Mom was a pioneer in this small town. When she returned to Marion after earning her medical degree in St. Louis, the population was only about 400 people. Some people may have believed she was nothing more than a glorified midwife, but those few, far, and in between criticisms didn't deter her from doing what she was trained to do; take care of women, their bodies, and their babies.

Back in those days, the late 1960s, the rest of the country might have been all about peace, love, and equality, but in Marion people's ways were hard to change. It took a while for Mom to be looked upon as the healer that she was. Her first waiting room was the front parlor of our farmhouse, long before I was born.

"What's voodoo?" I asked her one day when I was about five. It had been a rare Sunday when it was just her and I. Nobody was requesting her appearance to bring a new life into the world. Usually, I spent Sundays with Granny and Granddad at their house, which was technically on our farm but a couple of acres enough away that we didn't see them every day.

We were working in the garden, getting it ready to plant the first crops of the spring. By that time the farm was no longer a working farm, just miles and miles of land to be admired for its purity. The only farming we did was in a 12 foot by 12 foot plot in our backyard.

"Voodoo? Where did you hear that word?" Mom smiled as she dropped a pea seed into the tiny hole she had poked into the soft earth.

"Bobby Cullins," I replied. Bobby Cullins would be the bane of my existence for years. I just didn't know it yet. I heard Mom sigh, but she didn't respond. "So," I prodded. "What is it?"

"It's a type of spiritual magic that people from other cultures embrace as a way to another spiritual pathway." Mom had a way of speaking to me like I was her equal, even when I was too young to really understand what she was saying.

"Bobby says people use voodoo to hurt people."

"I guess people can use their thoughts or their religion to hurt people, but not in magical ways."

"Bobby says that his daddy says that you do voodoo when you help people."

Mom sighed again. Years later she would tell me that Bobby Cullins' dad had been a dim-witted asshole who believed women were merely meant to cower to a man's will. But that day she simply asked, "What do you think?"

I stopped my planting and looked up at Mom, her face a shadow as the sun shone behind her, illuminating her already fiery red hair, the same red hair that I had. I remember feeling the love spread through my body. I climbed into her lap, dirty and smelling like damp earth. "I love you, Mommy."

She held me tight and rocked me back in forth as we sat in the garden. "I love you, too."

***

"Charlotte?" the voice crept up behind me. By instinct I touched the back of my neck, running my fingers along the ridge of a scar that still tingled when I heard that voice, while my other hand touched my stomach. I turned slowly, willing myself to stand steady. I searched the crowd for Nick, but couldn't find him among the masses.

"Bobby." Unlike the majority of people in Marion, he hadn't aged much since the last time I saw him, a few months after high school graduation. The true townies, those who lived and died in Marion, tended to grow wider as the years passed. Their hair seemed to fade and they wore the hardships that farming can do to a soul on their faces. Not Bobby. He still looked the same nearly 20 years later. He must have gotten away from this town, too.

He tucked his hands into his pants pockets and regarded me with uncertainty. "Sorry to hear about your mom."

"Hmmm," that was all I had managed to say. I had better manners, but I couldn't conjure them at that moment.

"Thank you," Nick said for me. I closed my eyes and thanked Mom. She must have seen Bobby coming and sent Nick to rescue me because she couldn't. Nick took his place beside me and stared uncompromising at Bobby Cullins. For a moment I entertained a random thought. *I wonder if he goes by*

Robert now.

I started to excuse myself when a tow-headed child of no older than three came running past me, nearly knocking me to the ground. The little girl grabbed onto Bobby's legs and began tugging on his tailored pants. "This here is Annabelle," Bobby said, picking her up.

I tightened my grip on Nick's hand. He answered for me, us. "A beautiful little girl you have there."

Bobby nodded in agreement. The air was thick, chock-full of history and boiling with tension. I hadn't given much thought to him showing up here. It wasn't a secret that he wasn't my mom's favorite person (or mine) and he had rarely shown her much respect all those years ago. I suppose that people could change as the years wore on, growing into compassionate and decent human beings. But that scar still tingled, telling me to let Bobby and the past go. He had paid his respects and now it was time to leave.

"So, Charlotte," he started. "I was wondering if we could talk. I need to," he looked at Nick with uncertainty. "I wanted to apologize."

I found my voice. It came out gravely as if I hadn't muttered a word in all of my 36 years. "I think some things are best left alone."

"Maybe, but this matters too much. The way I treated you was wrong."

"I appreciate the sentiment, Bobby, but this isn't the place and I think it will do everyone well to leave the past where it belongs." I stared at that little girl whose almond-shaped brown eyes were staring at me too intently. "You do have a beautiful daughter."

***

The day had stretched itself out as long as it could. It seemed that the sun was unwilling to let Mom go, too. The visitors stayed until the sun bobbled just over the horizon; the last one to leave was Harold Klein. He hobbled over to me, leaning on his hand-carved cane with his hat in his hand. He seemed weak, defeated, and not like the man I remembered from all of those years past when he had stood on our front porch with the barrel of a gun lodged underneath his chin.

"Charlotte, I would ask how the day does you, but I suppose circumstances can speak for themselves." He didn't say the words unkindly. In fact, his voice seemed to catch as if he were holding back some complicated emotions I didn't really understand.

We stood next to the casket. I ran my hand over the polished wood wondering where my mother was. Not being a faithful person myself, I felt empty and unsure. Maybe if I had gone to church with Jia a few times I would have felt fulfilled and at peace knowing my mom was dancing in fields of gold, my father welcoming her with open arms. Then again maybe I wouldn't. "It's been a long day."

Harold nodded. "Yes. Yes, it has."

"You've been here for a long time, Mr. Klein. You must be tired."

"Live this long, dear, and everything will make you tired." He reached into his suit and pulled out an envelope. "I wanted to wait until everyone had left. You know how these places are. Towns like this. People like to talk."

I reached out to take the envelope, but he didn't let go right away. "You've turned out all right, I suppose – a spitting image of Sylvie. I'm sure you made her proud."

A smile tugged at the corners of my mouth even though his compliment was awkward. I hoped this was true. Mom and I were so different and some of the choices I had made haunted me. I wanted to believe that I hadn't failed her. Harold released his hold on the envelope and placed his hat on his head.

"Well, goodnight Charlotte. Read that over tonight. It's important. I will see you soon."

I watched him hobble off as Nick came up beside me. "What was that all about?"

I took a closer look at the letter and saw my mom's handwriting. The letter was addressed to me. We went inside the farmhouse and sat down in the living room in front of the fireplace. I wished it was colder. It was too hot to consider a fire, but I had always felt comforted by the crackling embers when we would fire up the fireplace during the winter months. Nick sat behind me on the tattered red couch and rubbed my shoulders. That couch was one of the few purchases my mom had made that wasn't a hand-me down. She never believed in buying something when you could reuse something else. She had been eco-friendly long before it was trendy.

As I opened the letter, I saw my mom's badly slanted writing. A leftie, her words always pulled to the left.

Dearest Charlotte,

In death life is revealed. Those left behind continue to tell the story. Memories and truths spill unrestrained. Death brings peace, but sometimes chaos. Never underestimate the power of truth over those who are living.

Waiting rooms tell stories. They are a medical purgatory. Some sit in the waiting room for hours to be shone the light, graced with blessings, like a new baby. For others this is the final holding room before they are delivered into hell, facing uncertainty, despair, sadness, even death. I spent my life opening the door to the waiting room; delivering a person's fate, dressed in a white coat, burdened by their pain, elated by their joy. I hid in that waiting room, too. I let the waiting room consume me and my failures.

There are still some stories left to tell. Unfortunately, if you are receiving this letter it is because I haven't been able to tell them to you. You need to know these stories because they are part of your life. Know that I love you more than my life. I am happy and at peace.

Always in Your Heart,

Mom

At the bottom of the letter was a post-it note with instructions:

Meet me in the waiting room tomorrow 9 am. Regards – Harold Klein

My hand trembled slightly as I handed the letter to Nick. "What do you think this means?" he asked.

I had an uneasy feeling. "I don't know," I whispered.

Nick slid down to sit next to me, encircling me in his arms. He rested his chin on my head and I closed my eyes. I loved moments like this when I felt protected. Too many times in my life I had felt vulnerable. "So, what do we do?"

"I guess we put this day to rest and then face tomorrow."

Chapter 2 – Harold
1945

She sat on the side of his front porch kicking her feet back and forth against the lattice that covered the crawl space. Clack. Clack. Clack. She kept staring at him, squinting into the sun and wrinkling her nose.

"You sure are one foul smelling creature." She laughed at her stupid joke.

He didn't say anything. Instead he plunged his hand into the bucket of well water to wet the bar of lye soap he was using to scrub the filth off his body. God blessed outhouse had decided to devour him when he was using it as a hideout. He should have known better than to play hide and seek with a bunch of sissy girls. That was just asking for trouble.

"I don't think it's working." Sylvie spoke in a singsong way as her feet continued to clack, clack, clack.

"Why don't you just go home?"

Sylvie shrugged. He looked up in the back window and saw Mabel sticking her tongue out at him, making crazy eyes. *Great*, he thought, *they trapped me inside and out.* Sylvie stopped mocking him for a while, but she didn't stop watching him. Nope. She sat there staring at him and fiddling with that nasty rag doll that she dragged with her everywhere.

It wasn't even a proper rag doll. It was more of a shit brown glob. Of course, Harold only knew what a proper rag doll looked like because Mabel had a whole bureau filled with them. That nasty thing didn't resemble anything close to Mabel's exquisitely designed dolls. But it wasn't like Sylvie could afford a proper doll. With her pops unable to secure steady work and with little skill to promote, it didn't look like she would ever be able to carry anything other than a shit brown glob. As he considered this he almost felt sorry for her. Then she opened her big mouth.

"Hear you been skinning cats."

"So?" He quickly stole a glance at the lattice, remembering that a couple of his trophies were rotting under there.

"You aren't worried about getting caught?"

He scrubbed at his skin harder. It didn't seem to make a difference. If anything it rubbed the filth into his skin even deeper, creating a deeper stink. "By who? You?"

"Anyone. Jimmy Barnes' cat went missing two nights ago. Saw him putting up flyers after he attended services this morning. He was nearly crying every time he asked if anyone had seen his precious Muttons."

"What kind of name is that for a cat?"

"A proper name."

He shrugged. "Mind your business, Sylvie."

"It's just wrong, Harold. Don't it make you sad to take a life? Take something that don't belong to you?"

Why didn't she just shut up? "Ain't my concern. Just a dumb animal. What you eat on your plate every night? You don't think that's the same?"

"It ain't the same, Harold. You better change your ways or you always gonna stink like shit."

With that she catapulted off the porch, letting that poor excuse of a rag doll bounce against her legs as she walked away. Sylvie Gold was nothing but a sour apple. She always looked at him with disdain like he wasn't any better than the dirt on her shoe, when she was the one who came from squalor and bad pedigree. Still he knew she had a point and it bugged him. Skinning cats was wrong. He knew he was breaking the commandments, but what else did a ten-year-old boy have to do?

Something else bothered him lately about the way Sylvie looked at him. Usually her meanie stares and uppity attitude didn't bother him, but something was changing. He found that it aggravated him that he cared what she thought. He even found himself experiencing the sensation that a million butterflies were fluttering around inside his stomach. He had considered confiding in Mabel about these weird sensations, but at the last second decided against it. Even then he knew it was better to suppress any feelings he had about Sylvie Gold.

In the summer of 1945 Harold Klein wanted nothing more than to play baseball. His dad bought him a signed Lou Gehrig ball at an auction on one of his business trips and he spent hours tossing it up in the air as high as he could and then running as fast as he could to catch it. He had no doubt that he would make the greatest outfielder the game had ever seen. Even though he knew girls didn't play baseball (although he suspected Sylvie might) he had even entertained the thought of asking Mabel to play catch with him, but that would be nothing but a waste of time. It was times like this when he wished he had been born the twin of a brother, not a stupid girl like Mabel because if the truth were to be told, Harold had a hard time making friends. He didn't have enough friends to make up a team much less to play catch with.

"Where are all your friends, son?" his father had asked one day when they headed down to Main Street after church.

Harold shrugged and drank his soda pop at the bar while his dad mingled with the businessmen and townsfolk of Marion. Harold hated Sundays. These were the days he was forced to face people. It wasn't that he didn't like people; they just didn't seem to care for him. He was awkward and shy. Not anywhere near as outgoing and personable as Harold Klein Sr., attorney at law. It wasn't that he didn't try to make friends; he just could never stomach enough interest in the same things as the boys his age. In a small town like Marion if you didn't care about county fairs, the price of corn, and whether or not it was a good growing season then you were considered an outcast.

Harold did have one person he could consider a friend of

sorts. Bart Cullins. Bart Cullins was not the kind of friend that good, God fearing boys hung out with, though. Bart Cullins was what most people would consider white trash. Then again many people considered Sylvie's pop white trash and Mabel still hung out around her. Harold figured things were different for girls.

"That Bart Cullins is not someone you should be hanging around with," Harold Sr. had mentioned the day Bart showed up at the house nosing around like he was looking for unsecured points of entry for future reference. The Cullins had a mean streak; perhaps some genetic default. There weren't too many people willing to get tangled up with that clan. *Maybe that is why I chose Bart to be my friend*, Harold reasoned. We are both outcasts in a community that breeds intolerance.

"He's my friend," Harold protested. The senior Harold didn't seem to have the heart to protest. Knowing that his son struggled to make friends, who was he to deny him this friendship? Of course, there was a perfectly good reason; especially if he knew that Bart was introducing his son to sadistic activities – like skinning cats.

The first time it disgusted Harold. As Bart began skinning it alive, the cat started to howl and whither under the blade. Harold couldn't bear it and he threw up all over his shoes. Bart merely laughed, shaking his head.

Harold had wiped the vomit dribble off his lips with the back of his hand, taking deep breaths. He looked around, suddenly very much aware that while they were behind Bart's house, they were still out in the open, clearly visible to anyone passing by. Bart lived in a two-bedroom shack adjacent to the hustle and bustle of Main Street. His home was observable by anyone interested in casting a scornful glance at the residence – as they often did. "Someone's gonna see," Harold whispered, trying not to lose what was left of his stomach contents.

Bart laughed. It was a bottomless laugh that sounded like it belonged to a criminally insane man – not a 10 year old boy. "Who cares? Besides, most people stay away from here. They know what's good for them." He waved the knife and laughed again.

"Your turn." He handed Harold the knife and gestured to the cat that lay withering at his feet.

"I don't want to," Harold asserted.

"Come on. It's just a cat."

Peer pressure was a social disease, even in 1945. What choice did Harold have? It was either submit to this cruel act or risk being ridiculed, denounced, and possibly skinned alive himself. No, there really was no choice. He had to do it.

Why Harold had continued to do it he couldn't say. It had been four months since he crossed that line with Bart for the first time. But he took no pleasure in skinning those cats. In fact, he cried each and every time he did it. Sylvie was right. What he did was much different than what the butchers did when the cattlemen bought their meat in to be processed. He was killing. They were surviving.

Harold believed in a way he was surviving, too, although *what* he was surviving, he wasn't quite sure. It wasn't as if his life was all that difficult. He lived comfortably with his father, mother, and Mabel. They always had food on the table. His parents weren't angry or hostile to each other or to their children. Their house wasn't like other houses where poverty and hostility went hand in hand. No, Harold didn't have much to feel sorry about. Yet he felt like each day was a struggle – a struggle to find his place in a community where he didn't feel at home.

***

The summer of 1945 seemed to last forever. The days were endless. The heat unrelenting. Everyone seemed to be having a hard time. Crops were suffering without the rain. Tempers were rising as quickly as the mercury in the thermometer. Women began to spend entire days doing nothing but sipping lemonade under the shade trees. Men forgot about the crops and spent too much time at home bothering their women. What this meant was come the New

Piper Punches

Year there were plenty of women walking around town with wide, swollen bellies.

Thankfully, Harold's mother had been spared. The heat hadn't touched their family in that way, but Sylvie's house was a different story. One day just before Thanksgiving, when Sylvie escaped from under her mother's watchful eye, Harold intentionally eavesdropped on a conversation between his sister and Sylvie.

"I think it's wonderful," Mabel had cooed.

"I guess." Sylvie responded.

"Why do you guess? Babies are so cute, cuddly, and they always smell delicious."

"Well, you don't eat babies. But, they sure need to eat."

"Oh."

Everything got quiet for a while. Then Mabel spoke again. "If you and your family need some food I am sure mother won't mind helping you out. We always have an extra loaf of bread and her jam is delicious. I'm sure mother would even let you put some food on her account at Mulligan's."

"I don't think Daddy would like that. He's proud."

"Yeah," Mabel agreed.

Harold had leaned against the wall, breathing slowly so he wouldn't be heard. Mabel had gotten use to his spying. He had to be pretty clever to elude her, but he didn't want to risk it. As Sylvie and Mabel started talking about some girl at school, Harold snuck away, but didn't stop thinking about what he'd overheard. An idea had begun to form. Maybe he could redeem himself for that cat business (which he had stopped shortly after Sylvie's intervention shamed him into doing the right thing). Perhaps he could be the person he knew he should be.

The trick was not to get caught. If Harold knew one thing it was that Gavin Gold was a proud man, just like Sylvie had said. He wouldn't take too kindly to handouts. He had survived the Depression (barely). He would insist he could survive this.

The problem with Sylvie's pops, Harold reckoned, wasn't

106

his lack of aptitude but mainly his inability to stop hitting the moonshine. This had cost him too many jobs, including a job working at the meat processing plant in town. Harold understood why they had to let him go. Meat grinding and intermittent soberness didn't make for a safe working environment. But being jobless and a drunk didn't put food on the table either and Sylvie's pop was a temperamental man. Not unreasonable, just a little unstable. You had to make sure you were on the right side of his mood.

That evening just before dinner, Harold snuck into the kitchen while his mother tended to one of Mabel's tantrum. Apparently, she been absently wandering about the yard and gotten one of her nice dresses caught on a splinter of wood that was sticking out of the entrance fence to their property. Now she was sniveling and carrying on. Usually, Harold would have been aggravated by this, but this time he took advantage of it.

He created a hammock with his front shirt tails and placed the bread for the evening meal into his pouch. He snatched a jar of jam from the canning pantry and, at the last second, grabbed a tea towel from the counter to wrap the contraband in when he delivered it. Next, he snuck around the side of the house to the chicken coop out back. His parents were far from the farming type, but they did keep a few chickens around for fresh eggs. Usually, there weren't eggs available this late in the day, but his mother must not have had time to collect them that morning. Two round eggs were waiting for Harold to pilfer. He wrapped everything in the tea towel and hid it underneath the crawl space. He'd take it to their house tonight when everyone was asleep.

Dinner was perplexing for Harold's mother. She stood over the stove, scratching and shaking her head. "That bread was sitting right here. I don't understand," she had said for the fifteenth time.

Harold Sr. laughed and reached across the table for a heap of mashed potatoes. "It's perfectly okay, Ellie. We all lose our mind eventually."

Harold's mother gave him a mischievous smile and waggled her finger at her husband. "I am not losing my mind. I baked two loaves of bread today. I can't imagine where the one for dinner went." This is when Mabel kicked Harold hard under the table, narrowing her eyes at him. He resisted the urge to make a face. The less attention drawn to him the better.

The Klein's house was two streets parallel to Main Street in town, which made it not quite a country house. But it backed up to a wide expanse of forest that separated the "townies" from the "countries." This is how most Marion residents referred to themselves, although visitors from larger cities like St. Louis would have found that description something to chuckle at because to these sorts of visitors the entire town was country.

Harold had begged off early after dinner complaining of a stomachache. "Hmph," Mabel had mumbled, but she left him alone. Now that it was dark the woods that separated his home from Sylvie's seemed menacing and foreboding. More than once he almost turned around and ran home, but he was determined to be the hero.

The thick blanket of forest was about two miles deep. On the other side of the towering oaks and massive maples were open fields as far as the eye could see. Sylvie's cabin sat right on the edge of the woods, where the fields and the trees met. Finally, after what must have been close to an hour of walking through the dark night he came within sight of the cabin. It was no wonder that Sylvie preferred to spend her days at his house playing with his insufferable sister. The cabin was falling apart at the seams. Although night had already fallen, it didn't prevent him from noticing the deteriorating conditions of the structure. The cabin was a poor excuse for a house. The metal roof was rusting in most places. Paint was peeling off the wood siding and there were several holes in the siding where mice and birds had begun to nest. The porch floorboards were riddled with holes too and the shutters hung crookedly off the hinges. Trash littered the yard and weeds grew up between old tires and other debris. He wondered if it even had electricity or modern conveniences like a stove or even an icebox. He marveled at how people could live without these contemporary necessities.

But a flame flickered in the window, casting a warm glow. He didn't want to get caught, so he stayed in the woods circling around the house until he found himself near the back door. He was pretty sure this was the door that led to the kitchen. If he sat the food on the single wooden step, it should be seen first thing in the morning. But then he realized a wild animal could come when he left and steal the whole lot. So he made a brave decision. He walked quietly to the back door, laid the bundle of food on the step, and knocked, hard and loud. Then he ran as fast as his feet would take him.

The next morning Harold was out in the backyard tossing a brand new ball his dad had given him. The air was unusually warm for November. He had on his heavy coat, but he was already starting to break a sweat. That's when he saw Sylvie emerge from the trees. In her hand was the bundle. Harold started to smile, proud to be recognized for his good deed, but stopped when he saw her nostrils flaring.

"Where's your sister?"

"I dunno. Why?"

"I told her not to do this." She looked down at the bundle in her hand.

"Mabel didn't do that."

"Then who? She's the only one who —" Sylvie stopped short. She glared at me. Her nostrils flared even wider. "You were eavesdropping."

"It's my house, too."

"That was a private conversation."

"What's the big deal? You needed food. I got you food. Why can't you be a normal person and just say thank you?"

"It is a big deal, Harold. This — " she held out her hands with the food bundle. "This could get us in serious trouble.

My daddy ain't like yours. He's proud and angry."

"Well, I'm sorry. But I heard your momma was having that baby and you guys didn't have food. What did you expect us to do?"

"Nothing. Absolutely nothing." She shoved the bundle into his stomach. Harold refused to take it and it dropped at their feet.

"You're being downright ungrateful. If this food will help, just take it. How's your pops gonna know?"

Sylvie was silent. She bit her bottom lip and plopped down on the ground. Her pants were worn and didn't look one bit warm. She pulled her knees in to her chest, resting her chin on top of them. Harold gathered up the bundle of food. One of the eggs had cracked, its gooeyness oozing onto the ground.

"Will your pops hurt you?" Harold asked.

Sylvie shook her head. "Not on purpose. He's angry, but not really mean. I think he's angry at himself because he sucks on that stupid drink all day long. He wants to take care of us and when he can't, it makes him sad. So he drinks to not feel sad but then he feels angry. It's confusing."

Harold didn't know what to say. He didn't have experience with this type of family dynamic.

"If Daddy knows that someone took care of us and he couldn't, he'll just keep drinking."

"But you can't starve."

"We ain't gonna starve." Sylvie stood up and gestured to the bundle. "It was nice of you to steal the bread and jam. But I can't take that."

Sylvie walked away in her threadbare pants, arms wrapped around her middle for warmth, head held high.

***

It happened a few weeks into the New Year. The townspeople claimed that they could hear the anguished cries coming from the Gold cabin in the wee hours of the morning; the hours of the night right before sunrise when it is the darkest and coldest. Of course, this is country folklore and gossip. No one would have been able to hear a sound. They wouldn't have heard the cries of a mother in labor. They wouldn't have been privy to whether or not Gavin Gold had been so mortified at the site of his son that he snuffed the life out of him. There is no way they could have known how desperately Sylvia had clung to her mother's weakening hand, urging her to push, begging her to stay with them.

Sylvie later recounted the circumstances of that night to Harold, years after the incident. She told him that after an exhaustive labor, Laurel Gold lay in the sweat and blood soaked bed, lifeless and gone. The baby boy had been born into the world silent. Sylvie and her dad had delivered him, but it was clear from the beginning that the baby was wrong.

"Mongoloid," Gavin had whispered or maybe it was *monster.* Sylvie couldn't remember. She only knew that she had to preserve a moment with this little baby, who had for a brief second been her brother. She held him in her arms, kissed his head, and rocked him as her mother would have.

For what seemed like hours Sylvie had held onto the baby, while her mother lay on the death bed and her father slumped against the wall with his head in his hands. Eventually, they buried the baby together. He was never given a name. He was buried in her mother's arms on the cabin's property. In one night two lives disappeared. One had no record of death; the other no record of life.

Sylvie only recounted this tale one time in her life then never spoke of it again.

ACKNOWLEDGEMENTS

I want to take a moment to thank my readers. You have embraced me and welcomed me into your personal libraries. You have allowed me to entertain you with my stories. This is something that I never for one second dismiss or take for granted.

I must also, once again, thank my husband, Tom, for his support because writing a book isn't only a solitary adventure for the writer, but for their family as well. There are days when he may have wondered when I would emerge from the office and nights when he wondered when I would come to bed. I am also thankful that he still wants to sleep next to me at night when he reads what I write. I am almost always certain he sleeps with one eye open.

Again, let me take a moment to thank the two people that have helped me create a book I am proud to share with the masses. My editor, Kristina, is never afraid to challenge me and offer constructive feedback. Her input is invaluable. Thank you, Kristina.

I also have to thank my cover designer, Marty. He learned first-hand what it can be like to work with me and just how picky I can be. I could promise things will change, but let's be honest . . . they won't.

That about sums it up. I'll be back soon with a brand new book and a million more reasons to say thank you!

ABOUT THE AUTHOR

Piper Punches lives in the far west suburbs of St. Louis with her husband and two daughters. Piper is excited to connect with her readers and encourages everyone to stop by her website and say hello. In the meantime, she is currently working on her second novel, *60 Days*, which will be available in the spring of 2014. She is also the author of *The Waiting Room*.

CONNECT WITH PIPER PUNCHES

http://www.piperpunches.com

http://www.facebook.com/piperpunches

http://www.twitter.com/piperpunches

http://www.goodreads.com/piperpunches

Have you read The Waiting Room?

Now's your chance to read the first two chapters of this

breathtaking debut novel available on Amazon.com

www.ingramcontent.com/pod-product-compliance
Lightning Source LLC
Chambersburg PA
CBHW030642130626
46552CB00002B/984